A Rumour
of Otters

A Rumour
of Otters

Deborah Savage

Houghton Mifflin Company
Boston 1986

Library of Congress Cataloging-in-Publication Data

Savage, Deborah.
  A rumour of otters.

  Summary: Angry at being left behind when her father
and brother go off to muster sheep, Alexa decides to
search in the wild for the otters previously seen only
by a mystical Maori tribesman.
  [1. Otters—Fiction. 2. New Zealand—Fiction]
I. Title.
PZ7.S2588Ru   1986   [Fic]   85-24818
ISBN 0-395-41186-6

First American edition 1986
Copyright © 1984 by Deborah Savage
Published in the United States by Houghton Mifflin Company
First published by William Collins Publishers Limited Auckland N.Z., 1984

Printed in the United States of America

s 10 9 8 7 6 5 4 3 2 1

A Rumour
of Otters

1

THE FROST CRYSTALS cut into Alexa's skin as she pressed her face against the dark window. Her breath felt hot on her mouth and the frost turned to beads of water as she stared out into the dark morning. She could just make out the figures of her father and the other men beginning their preparations for the autumn muster. The moisture on the window warped her vision, and the figures seemed wavy and ghost-like in the dim light. It was late autumn in the South Island, and the nights already brought frosts that laced the rough tussock grass and covered the fence-posts until mid-morning. The tin roofs on the farm sheds, faded red by searing summer sun and violent winters, seemed to quiver in the early morning with their covering of frost reflecting the warm light streaming from the kitchen downstairs.

Alexa heard her mother calling Tod, and her quickened breath made angry circles in the frosted glass. Tod was her brother. Her mother's voice reminded her of the reason she still had not gone downstairs into the early morning house. She wanted nothing to do with the rest of the family, and especially not with Tod.

She snorted in disgust. The way her mother had called him just then — it was the same voice she used with the men, with her father even! As if Tod were a man! She angrily scraped the frost from the corners of the window, so as to see as much of the yard below her as possible. Yes, there he was, and each stride he took towards the house pumped up Alexa's anger.

Tod was *not* a man. He was just sixteen — barely two years older than herself.

'I ride just as well as you!' she whispered fiercely into the darkness. 'And Dad knows it! And I can whistle up the dogs as good, and I'm as strong as you . . .' She heard a door slam and someone coming up the stairs; she threw herself back into the still-warm bed and squeezed her eyes shut.

Without knocking, Tod opened the door and came in.

'Come on, Lex!' he cried, his voice high with excitement. 'Don't you want to help me get my stuff ready? Dad said to ask if you'd help oil the bridles. Come on! Why're you still in bed?' He reached out and flicked at the woollen blankets covering the lumped form of his sister. There was no response. Deflated for a moment, he turned toward her desk, riffled through the papers and books lying there.

The form on the bed suddenly came to life.

'Stay *out* of that!' Alexa cried. 'I mean it! Don't you ever touch what's on my desk!' She sat tautly in the bed and stared at her brother. 'And don't you believe in knocking?' she flung at him.

'Well what's the matter with you?' Tod muttered. What a bore Alexa had become, and she used to be fun, ready for anything. Lately, though, there had been nothing but sullen looks from her, avoiding his eyes, or sudden explosions, like this one. He shook his head heavily, as if to clear it of something he didn't understand.

'Come on, Lex,' he pleaded. 'We could go for a ride — after I get my gear ready, I mean. Don't you want to?'

How to explain to him? She really didn't care, anyway. If he couldn't figure out what was the matter, who wanted to explain! But the frustration and disappointment pressed uncontrollably at her throat. If she didn't say something, she might cry. She clenched her fingers under the covers.

'Who wants to ride with you?' she said, her voice steady. 'You're going off on the muster anyway — you'll get all the riding you want, and with your mates, too. If I'm not good enough to go muster, I don't see why I'm good enough to ride with you at all!' This last was flung out illogically, she knew.

8

They looked at each other in silence.

'Why, *why* won't Dad let me go?' she cried at last, and her voice came out a cracked whisper. Tod stuffed his hands deep into his pockets. He leaned against the desk and pushed over a pile of books; the movement made him spring forward, and stand as if to attention. He wished he'd just left his sister to sleep.

It was four days ago that Jim had announced at tea: 'Well, Tod, I reckon I need another hand this year. What do you say?' It was what he'd been waiting for, holding his breath for. It was, in a way, why he'd quit school. And now, at last, to go on the autumn muster, the annual gathering of all the station's sheep from the almost impassable mountains and to bring them slowly back to lower blocks for winter keeping! The muster could take several days, in the most rugged terrain and often under severe conditions: an early winter snow, high winds, the danger of injury to men, horses or dogs . . . Thinking of it made his breath catch in his throat with excitement.

And now he remembered something else from the joy of Jim's announcement four days ago: Alexa's face, strained, eager, waiting . . . and the blankness which followed, Jim didn't extend an invitation to her. She was not to go.

Now, he struggled to say something. She was challenging him to answer, with her dark face glowering over the woollen blankets, her hair mussed, her face hot.

'I — I don't know,' he mumbled at last. 'Well, hell, Lex! When'd you ever see a lady musterer? You ought to know girls don't ride off. You have to stay in huts with all the men — you know you can't . . .' He'd started off strongly, but his voice trailed helplessly.

'Don't be daft!' Alexa sat up straight in bed, levelling her deepest attack. 'You know I can ride as good as you, I can even beat you. I know this station as well as you do — probably better. You haven't even been around for two years, off in that poncey school!'

Tod stomped out, slamming the door behind him. It didn't latch, and when he turned to slam it again, Alexa called after him, 'You don't want me to go 'cause you know I'm as good as you, an' you wouldn't want your mates to see that!' She sneered the word *mates*.

She couldn't stay in the room now, feeling this angry restlessness. She picked up the pile of books which had fallen from her desk, and pushed the papers back into a pile. Her school assignment lay on top, reviving a nagging worry of the last few weeks. She had assured her parents that if they allowed her to continue her schooling through the correspondence programme, rather than being sent off as Tod had been to a private school in the city, that she would do her school work without being told, and she would keep up her studies without prodding. Seeing the assignment on her desk relieved some of the pressure of the last few minutes with Tod, but replaced it only with a sharp worry. The instructions from her science teacher, sent through the mail a few weeks ago, had been clear: research and compose a paper on an endangered animal in New Zealand. She hadn't even started, and it was the main assignment of the term.

'I just can't stay here today!' she said aloud in the cold room. Everything pushed at her: the anger at Tod and her father, and this school assignment. In sudden decision, she grabbed some papers from her desk, pencils, an old scruffy notebook, and stuffed them into her rucksack. She padded softly down the back stairs after dressing herself in warm clothes. She had to sneak by the kitchen, and she saw Marty feeding the baby in the short lull between cooking and waiting for the men to come in for breakfast.

The grass crinkled softly under her feet as she moved towards the dark paddock. The flurry of activity centred on the far end of the yard, where the sheds were, so no one saw her. She knew every rock, every hollow and rise in this paddock. The shadows breathing in the far corner were darker than the night, and they stirred, becoming horses. They raised their heads at the girl's approach, muttering through rubbery lips and from deep within their chests. She ran her hand along their rough backs, feeling the coarse fur which was the beginning of their winter coats. The bones of

10

the shoulders, the strong ridges of the ribcage — all that she could feel under the dark coats.

Here was Nelson; he was hers. His nose was warm and like velvet against her hand. She led him out, smoothed his mane, slipped the bridle over his ears. He was not surprised to see her. Often, as early as this, the girl would take him out over the low hills that surrounded the station buildings and the homestead. He liked these early morning expeditions; the air was cool.

This morning, the girl was tense. The horse shifted uneasily next to her. She was in a hurry. She whispered to him.

'C'mon! C'mon, Nelson! Don't be cheeky this morning!' She tugged at his rein and he followed to the gate, his unshod hooves hushed thuds on the cold earth. She left him there, and he stood, head up, waiting by the gate while she opened it.

Alexa looked anxiously towards the movement of men, saw her father lugging a large sack in the direction of a low shed. If he saw her, he would be sure to call out, give her some chore to do, something in preparation for the muster. The muster, which she could not go on. Quickly and surely, she led Nelson through the gate, latched it, and jumped up on his back. She clasped him with long, strong legs and urged him into a canter. She looked back; no one had seen them. Good. Alexa let out her breath suddenly, seeing it form a cloud in front of her face. It was cold. Nelson wanted to run, so she let out his rein and leaned low over his neck.

Very quickly, they left behind the clipped grass and neat buildings. The station was not a prosperous one and had very little flat grassland. The terrain turned abruptly into hills, covered in tussock, matagouri, tea tree scrub. There were patches of aspens running up the hollows near the closer paddocks, and later, beech forests struggled for a hold on the rock and scree-covered slopes. Goats and wild deer had ravaged many of the forests, and some of them died altogether, leaving great scars of dead trees on the lower slopes.

Alexa gave Nelson his head. He had been born and raised in this land, knew the loose shale under his feet, knew the great thorns of the matagouri scouring his belly. And he knew his rider. They always went the same way on these early rides. He flexed his neck, arched his tail, flew up the ridge and out along a low saddle. It banked sharply down into a gully filled with tussock and scrub, but there was a wide sheep trail through it. The horse thundered along it.

Alexa gulped the wind bashing against her face and felt some of the sharpness of anger leave her. The cold morning felt good slicing through her clothes. If she let Nelson full out the whole way she would make it to Belson's Saddle by sunrise. She leaned low over his neck. Every sensation felt accentuated, the sharpness of wind, the strong muscles between her legs, feeling the ground up through the back of the horse until she felt it was she galloping.

Belson's Saddle rose ahead of her. From here in the low gully it seemed impassable, but she knew there was a narrow sheep track zig-zagging up it, and from the top the station became a toy and all around it, as far as the eye could see, were dun-brown ridges and dark shadowed gullies until at last the eye hit the vast white mass of the Kaikoura mountains. Nelson slowed at the foot of the saddle, picking his way carefully up the shale. Tussock grew here and there, making the earth firmer, and Alexa shifted her weight into her knees to give the horse more leverage.

The morning was a bright grey by now, but the sun had not yet shot above the mountains. On the saddle top, the horse stopped, lathered, breathing heavily from red nostrils. Alexa, too, was out of breath, and her legs trembled as she stood. No matter how many times they did this, it was always five minutes before the heart stopped pounding, before the eyes cleared of pumping blood.

She sat braced against a rock. Below and beyond her, the world spiralled out in never-ending mountains. It was all dun and brown, grey and gold, rock, sky and mountain. Far below her somewhere, a kea screamed, and another answered. Above her, came the sharp clear note of a pipit in

12

the vast sky. And always the wind, defying the silence of the open spaces. She took out her notebook and the papers crammed into it, and waited.

The show was about to begin. Far beyond her, on the horizons of the world, marched the infinite sharp wall of the Kaikoura Range. Even at night, from her bedroom window, the whiteness blazed, dimming the stars. In mid-summer, the whiteness was relentless, uncompromising, always winter. Such a vast wall, such a vast distance away; Alexa felt the sharp jab of the peaks and ridges as if she were in that unending cold now. She could not think how old those mountains must be, they seemed so strong, and it always fascinated her to watch, as now, that strength tremble and shatter for a moment under the rise of a new day.

For now the white was infused with colour, with oranges, pinks and mauves. The mountains seemed to glow from within. From every part of the homestead, the Kaikouras dominated vision. Alexa caught her breath at the speed with which the face of the mountains moved, changed colour, opened. She could feel the warmth of the sun blast into her as it blasted that rim of mountains, feel it stealing over and through her, and making her at once as huge as those ranges, as small as the tiniest pebble. She wanted to spread her arms open to receive it all and grinned to herself at the impulse. Instead she settled herself against the rocks where she felt sheltered from the still-cold wind, and happily spread her rucksack out with all its contents. She would not be bothered here, it was her place. She could do, say, think what she wanted, say it aloud, and only Nelson, the keas, or the dusty brown lizards would hear.

She decided to think about Billy. She opened her notebook to a page of smudged pencil drawings, rough, awkward renderings of an old man in slouch hat, and a few snaky, long animals in the margins. At certain places among the pages were drawings of more recognisable things: Nelson, a sharp black-and-white collie dog, a gnarled tree. But the old man was drawn again and again, inexpertly, much-erased and over-drawn. This was Billy.

13

He was so old, he'd always been old, a Maori shearer who had appeared and disappeared in the lives of her family ever since she could remember, turning up for lambing or shearing. He had been everywhere, all over the South Island, probably all over the North as well. He told stories which always made the hired men laugh, slapping each other's backs. Tod would laugh too, as if *he* could understand, and her mouth pursed in a sneer remembering this.

But there was that one story he seemed always to tell just for her. It was the story of the otters. He would tell Alexa the story many times during one visit, if she asked him. His dark eyes would grin at her out of his old face.

She stared down at her drawings, wishing she could capture more clearly the images she saw when she listened to the story of Billy Turoa.

'One day, I saw him,' Billy would begin. No matter how the story changed from telling to telling, he always began it that way. One day, he saw him.

'One day, I saw him. He is *kaurehe,* serpent-dog; he is the one-who-wrinkles-water,' Billy would continue, and those words would enter Alexa's mind and form themselves into brilliant pictures. She saw the lakes of the high country, hidden in gullies, cold, far back in the mountains where only wild sheep could go. She saw the old man on a horse, and she saw what he had seen: the smooth surface of the lake broken by a sleek hump which moved without sound or splash through dark water. And she saw, as he had, the creature stop, raise its broad head high out of the water to look up at the rider sitting his horse, high above on the windy ridge.

'It was an otter,' Billy would state flatly, never minding the guffaws of the men around. But *she* believed him. She knew he'd seen something. She knew it could not be a fish; fish did not swim in that way. Nor a water bird, for the same reason. But mostly, she wanted, she *wanted* it to be an otter. Over many tellings of the story, the images had swum into her secretly, surely quiet like an otter itself. Over and over, she tried to capture in drawings the litheness and beauty of what she saw in her mind's eye, but she was never satisfied.

14

Further on in the little notebook were a few scribbled lines, attempts at a poem describing Billy's otter, and that, too, was unsatisfying.

There were no otters in New Zealand. Everyone knew that there were no indigenous wild mammals at all, apart from bats. Everything that ran the hills now was imported, the deer, the goats, pigs and sheep, the chamois, rabbits, weasels — all pests, all brought from far, far away, so far that Alexa's thoughts scrambled thinking of it. She read about places, in books, full of wildlife, full of creatures part of a place, their lives intertwined with the people in their legends, in their stories. It made her feel strangely lost, in a place at once infinite and tiny, stuck in the middle of the endless Pacific, even though she had been born here.

Beside her the horse shifted and rattled the bridle. She stood up and rubbed his forehead absently, leaning against the big warm neck.

'Oh, Nelson, there's nothing that's really *mine* here,' she said, and the big animal pushed at her with his head. 'Even you really belong to Dad. And Max . . .' She shook her head and decided not to think about the big dog tied down at the homestead, *her* dog, a possession threatened by Jim.

'I'll figure out about Max later,' she promised herself, aloud. Then, 'I bet there *are* otters out there,' she said, staring out into the mountains. 'I could take you and go, Max would help me — I could go . . .' She sighed and sat back down in her sheltered rocks, looking disgruntled as she studied the drawings in the notebook. She turned to the last section of the book. A letter was stuck between the pages, and she read it for the third time.

'Dear Alexa,' it read. The handwriting of her science teacher was always crabbed, as if written in a hurry. 'Thank you for writing about the idea for your paper. I am sure you will write a good one, as you are an excellent student. But I am afraid writing about otters does not fall into the category I have asked for. I did say *endangered,* not non-existent! The story your father's shearer told you is indeed colourful, but the idea of otters living in high country lakes, or anywhere in

15

New Zealand, is highly unlikely . . .'

And in that stingy style Alexa disliked, the letter went on to describe exactly what the teacher wanted.

'Why doesn't she just write it herself, she's not at all interested in what I want to say!' growled the girl. She felt the teacher's rejection of the otter story to be a slur against Billy.

She stuffed the letter back into the notebook. It was a problem, that paper — she could not seem to write it, unless it could be about otters.

The wind shifted, and the muted sound of a truck starting up, the shrill whinny of a horse, brought her back to the present. She stood up, dumping her notebook and papers into the old rucksack. Below her to the left, she could make out tiny figures in the now-bright morning, moving about the yard. The world had intruded and he no longer felt peaceful; she had to go back.

Her mother, Marty, met her at the kitchen door, her face red from the stove. She said nothing about her absence at breakfast. She seemed harried; the burden of feeding the six extra men hired for the muster showed on her face. She was carrying the three-month-old baby on her hip, and handed her over to Alexa. When the men and Jim left for the muster, Marty would be left to run the immediate station alone. Alexa felt a brief pull of guilt at wanting to go with the men; how could she leave her mother with everything? But stubbornly she retained her anger. She was not interested in her mother's kitchen, she did not feel anything for the baby, and the thought of being left to clean chook pens, milk cows, and the hundred other boring little chores that had to be done, while Tod and everyone were out in the mountains doing exciting things — it stuck in her throat. She looked at her mother over the milk-smell and dampness of the baby. Didn't she ever want to go? Didn't she at least know how much her daughter wanted to — couldn't she *tell*? Her mother could persuade Jim, if she wanted to.

'Lexa, would you watch the baby? I've got to sit for a while; I swear those men are always hungry. And the dogs need feeding . . .'

16

Alexa shifted the baby roughly to her other hip, hating the way she felt bony and awkward every time the baby was given to her. She dropped her rucksack on to the kitchen table and it broke open, spilling out papers. Marty poked at them with her fingers, smiling.

'Still having trouble with that paper?' she asked.

'I just can't think what to write, I guess,' mumbled Alexa. She wished her mother wouldn't be so nice, not when she herself felt so nasty. Her nastiness increased as Tod came in.

'Write about keas. They're endangered — 'specially when I've got my gun handy!' suggested Tod, having heard his mother's question. 'Sheep-killers . . .'

'Oh, they don't *kill* sheep. They just eat the ones that have already died, and you know it!' shot back Alexa. She didn't want to talk about the paper, certainly not with Tod around.

'That's not such a bad idea,' said Marty. 'You could really be a scientist, because you could go out and study them for real instead of just reading about them.'

'But I want to write about . . .' Alexa stopped, squirming against the counter with the weight of the baby. She hadn't meant to talk about it.

'What?' asked Marty.

'Well,' Alexa stumbled with the words. 'Billy Turoa used to tell me about, you know, otters. Didn't he ever tell you? I figured if he really saw one, they must be endangered . . .'

Tod gave a loud laugh, just as he did when Billy told the story. Alexa felt a burning in her eyes. Stupid, stupid! She *knew* she shouldn't have said anything. Tod used to be fun to talk to; he used to really talk to her. Now, ever since he came back from school and especially since knowing he was going to muster, all he ever did was jeer at her.

'Oh, shut up!' she flashed at him, turning to stalk from the kitchen.

'It's not such a silly idea,' Marty chided Tod. 'It's a long shot, but there're lots of ways otters could have got here. The Arabs were great sea explorers and they tamed otters to fish for them. Who knows, they could have explored this part of the Pacific, bringing their otters just like we take dogs with us.' Alexa had stopped, listening despite herself. Her mother might understand a *little* . . .

Tod plonked himself into a chair by the table and reached for an apple. What amazing ideas his mother had sometimes! Where did they come from? Arabs! Otters! And Alexa — she could always go off like that, too, talk about weird things, that had nothing to do with anything. He felt for a second lost, left out, as if something had suddenly moved past him. He didn't say anything for fear of appearing stupid, while Alexa glared at him from the doorway. He didn't meet her eyes.

'After everyone leaves, Lexa, we'll go over that paper. It's not such a silly idea, the otters, but it might be hard to research,' continued Marty, standing up again and turning to the counter. 'Now, I really need the dogs fed, and try to keep Emmie happy for a while.' Once again her voice sounded tired, distant. Alexa left with the baby. Once in a while, just once in a while, she felt she could talk to Marty; once in a while, her mother would open up — but the moment would pass quickly, for the demands of her work kept her busy.

The dogs were hungry. They had been sensing the growing activity for days and they were restless. Alexa was deaf to the cacophony of barking which greeted her appearance with the tucker pail. These were her father's working dogs. She admired their rough beauty, the strong bones prominent under shaggy coats, the bright ears pricked, listening for *his* voice, his command. They lived only to work, and she could not allow herself to love them. They were not meant to be loved but to be used, and they thrived on that barren allowance as her father thrived on the sparse land of the station. The massive huntaways leapt at the kennel fencing, their great block heads catching the morning light. The smaller, slender eye-dogs, the little black and white collies, stood silently among the noisy huntaways, taut and alert. Alexa measured out the dried kibble and table scraps into pails.

At the end of the row of kennels was Max, *her* dog. She

stubbornly thought of him as hers, although that possession was tenuous and threatened. Earlier in the morning, on her ride, she had not been able to face the problem. Now, with the dog standing waiting for her, she could not dismiss it. Max's eyes never left the girl, but he lay quietly while the others barked around him. He was already at ten months a huntaway of immense size and dense coat. His fur was less unkempt than his kennel-mates, for Alexa brushed him secretly with a horse brush, away from her father's eyes. The fur on Max's head was soft like gold velvet, and his brown eyes were set deep in the great head. She stared at him sadly. He was 'ruined', her father said. He was of no use to him. The great dog was afraid of sheep.

Alexa's father had selected Max as the most promising pup out of a litter by his best bitch. How he could have distinguished one squirming puppy from another, Alexa didn't know. It was part of the knowledge her father had which she wished she shared, but which she also feared because it made him so inaccessible to her. It was that knowledge that made his selection of the pup the right one; it was the same knowledge that gave him the right to kill it. Jim was always the one to do the killing of things; he killed the old chickens, shot lamed horses, privately killed the working dogs which had grown too old to work. Alexa always hated him as he went off to do the job, but when he came back, she would sneak a look at his face, and it was as if she had invaded his privacy, so intensely would the repulsion and sorrow show.

And now, after having chosen Max, he was going to kill him, too.

'I *can't* have a useless dog here, you know that!' he had said to her last week. 'I've given him a good long time to come right, and I don't see any sign he will. He isn't even happy, Lexa, without a job to do!' And he had left with his face closed to further discussion. She slammed the door of a kennel now, remembering. It was all her father's fault anyway, why Max was the way he was. He thinks you're only happy if you have a useful job to do, she thought in disgust. And it's all his fault.

She remembered Jim's eagerness six months ago when he tried out his new pup. Even at so young an age Max had shown signs of willingness and speed. Jim had gently picked the fat pup up in his big hands, speaking encouragement, and deposited him in a small pen with a dozen sheep, five of which had been young rams. Max had rallied beautifully, bracing his stubby legs in the yellow dust, approaching the animals with a mature sureness. Once near to them, he had begun to bark, calmly, but with puppy shrillness. Jim had grinned with pleasure. But the pup, like any good pup, had become over-eager, dashing into the mob, barking excitedly. Against the fence, the rams had turned to face him. He was too close to them now and uncontrolled. They sensed the man had no control over this dog, and stamped, charged, butting at the pup. Aggressive, they were not content with a warning, but pursued him. In the small pen, choked now with dust, Max was confused; he panicked, wet the ground, and the rams closed in again, stamping him. In the confusion, Jim reached the screeching pup, scooped him up and soothed him. Alexa, sitting tense on the fence, saw the pup stiffen in her father's hands, all trust of people gone, and she longed to hold him herself.

Max could never be persuaded to go near sheep after that. No matter what Jim did, with all his knowledge of dogs, the puppy would cower, whimper, wet the ground. In disgust and disappointment, one day, Jim shoved the pup at Alexa as he stalked out of a paddock, saying, 'Here, you take him till I figure out what to do with him.' She took the pup as a gift, wanting it as much because it was her father who had given it as for the pup itself. Even then, she had had a sense of the outcome. Her father kept nothing on the station he could not use.

She loved Max fiercely, all the more so because she was his only protection. She tried half-heartedly herself to work him with sheep, but gave up. If she had succeeded, he would have gone back to her father. Since she failed, and the dog persisted in his fear, he would have to be got rid of.

She knelt by the big animal now and buried her hand deep

in the thick ruff. Max was hers, more than anything else. She could not allow anything to happen to him. She would not. Somehow, this resolve connected with the immediate anger of being left out of the mustering, connected with Tod's taunting her about the otter idea. She felt tears burst in her eyes, and she rubbed them furiously. Max squirmed closer to her. If only she could go away from here, she felt such an outsider.

Her father appeared at the other end of the kennel to get some dogs. She scrambled to her feet. He smiled at her.

'Have a good ride this morning?' he asked, as he unlatched the gate. Was it possible he didn't even know how upset she was? That he could speak to her so casually? She studied his face. It was as it always was, lined, preoccupied, absently pleasant.

'Yes,' she answered at last. She wished she could say something to him, explain reasonably why she thought she should be allowed to go, why Max should be allowed to live, why, why, why — sometimes they would have a short conversation. Sometimes he would talk with her about things that she cared about and she would be so caught in the thrill of it that her words would stumble and she would feel awkward. He seemed he might talk now. She started towards him. Max bounced up. At the sight of the huntaway, a frown crossed Jim's forehead, his face closed, and Alexa, shielding the dog with her body, felt the light go out of the morning. She turned and went.

2

SPARKS SPAT OFF red-hot metal as the blacksmith hammered out shoes from a tiny forge on the back of a truck. Alexa sat watching on a fence post, while in the dust below her Max panted uncomfortably in the heat. It no longer seemed as if winter were approaching; the day had become as hot and dry as mid-summer. The musterers' horses stood loosely tethered, switching their tails in boredom, ignoring the hissing of hot metal in the bucket.

Max shone in the sun. His thick coat gleamed, as rich and polished as fine bronze. Alexa had spent an hour brushing him vigorously, and Max had been tolerant, perhaps sensing that she needed the activity. He was a strong dog, big-boned, muscled from the long runs he took besides Alexa's horse, and she loved to discover that strength under the bear-like coat. From the fence post, she trailed her foot along the dog's back and sighed, her face sweating from the forge. She was bored. She was the only one with nothing to do in the midst of activity.

Nothing around the station suited her. The thought of Marty in the house, fixing endless meals, feeding the baby, washing up, repelled her. She wanted to keep her mother company, but could not bring herself to go into the world of the kitchen. At any other time, the bustle of the sheep men around her in the yard, the smells of oiled leather, the coarse laughter and the sight of sweating, lifting, riding, inspired her with keen excitement. At one time, watching things

22

about to happen occupied her totally; but now this action had nothing to do with her. She shifted uncomfortably on the post.

The blacksmith pulled a pulsing red shoe from the fire, hammered it, sparking, and then dipped it with a hiss into the water. He fitted it to the horse's hoof. Alexa watched him nail the shoe on to the great cracked hoof, his hands deft, the extra nails sticking from his mouth like fangs. When she was younger, Alexa would cringe at that first hammering, feeling her own foot writhe and jerk each time a nail was driven in. But the horses never stirred. It had been a long time before Alexa had accepted reassurances that they felt no pain.

When the blacksmith went for his cup of tea, Alexa slid off the fence and wandered into a shed where Tod sat oiling a martingale strap. The bottle of leather oil had tipped into the dirt, leaving a dark stain. She set it upright. Neither of them spoke. Alexa dribbled soft dirt slowly over the puddle of oil, to soak it up.

'You want to go for a ride?' she asked finally. She clapped her hands free of the dirt vigorously, to hide the eagerness she felt. 'Bing's already shod, so we could get the pack horses. You want to?'

It wasn't Tod's fault she wasn't to go on the muster. It was just easier to yell at *him;* she couldn't betray her bitter frustration to Jim. Say you'll go riding with me, she pleaded silently. We could race. I'll let you win.

Tod grunted at her, rubbing the rough leather. He shook his head.

'You can finish that tonight,' she said, pleading in spite of herself, but Tod only poured more oil into his hands. Alexa kicked at the bottle.

'Dad didn't say you had to work all day!' she cried. The bottle overturned and Tod yelled at her, throwing the mass of straps down.

'You just want those men to see you!' She kicked the leather straps into a tangle. She wished more than anything she could sit with Tod and help him oil the gear. But what for? She wasn't going to use it.

23

'You think those guys are your *mates*?' she jeered. 'I bet they don't even care about you. You're just a kid!' Tod stood, stung, wanting to punch her.

'Yes they do!' he replied furiously. 'Dad wouldn't have asked me if he didn't reckon I'd be a help. Anyway, Dad wouldn't have anyone who wasn't any use along . . .'

Tod stopped, confused. The look on his sister's face frightened him. Why did he always manage to say something wrong, make her look that way? Once he'd shot a young red deer stag and wounded it. Panicked, he'd dashed towards it, wanting to help it, crying out at the pain he'd caused. But the stag had stared at him and he was unable to approach it, for it would have raked him viciously with its antlers. Alexa was like that now. What could he say to her that wouldn't cause her to lash out, to hurt him with her words the way no one else could? He was afraid of her.

'I know you'd be as good as me, on the muster,' he said at last, in a low voice, his throat tight. But Alexa didn't answer, stood staring at him. It encouraged him to go on, and suddenly, in a rush, the words came, everything he needed her to know.

'You always were as good as me, riding and such. 'Specially now, since I got back from school, because I didn't get much chance to ride or anything, there.' He stopped for a second. How could he explain?

'It's just that, well, if we *both* went, you know, we'd be *Jim's kids* . . . I mean, they wouldn't really pay attention to us, and I want them to see that I'm no longer a little kid.' Tod stumbled through the words. They had always been on equal terms, he and Alexa. They learned to ride together; they explored the station together. They competed, won and lost equally. Why, now, did he need to create a gulf between them?

'Someday I'm going to run the station, Lex! I have to know what's going on! The men have to listen to me! I'm sixteen! I'm a *man* now!' Tod felt tears just under the surface, and now somehow, it didn't matter if she saw them. She was standing in the shadow of the back wall, still, holding the end of the martingale strap as if frozen.

24

'I wish you could go, really!' He was telling the truth. He wished there were not these strange new rules in his life, separating his world from his sister's. 'But what d'you want to for? I mean, what good's it going to do you? You aren't going to stick around here; you *can't*.'

Her voice was a whisper. 'Why can't I?'

'Well, you know, maybe . . . well, one day you might get married or maybe you'll go travelling to Europe or America!' He got caught up in his enthusiasm, and Alexa, despite herself, grinned.

'You're daft!' she muttered, wanting to understand him. They stared at each other in the dim, cool light of the shed. He reached for the tangled straps and she gave them to him.

'Why don't you go ahead. If I have time, I'll catch up — you going the usual way?' he said.

She nodded. She realised he was embarrassed now, as if he'd said too much. She couldn't feel any anger toward him. Suddenly, she welcomed the thought of another ride alone, when only minutes ago the loneliness of the day seemed more than she could bear. Perhaps, after all, he would catch up to her, they could race, Nelson and Bing, along the narrow sheep trails . . . but later, later after she'd thought about things awhile.

She left the shed, left Tod bent once again over the straps of leather. From the doorway, looking back, she thought how like Jim he looked, for that instant. He had the same tired, patient bend in his back, the same frown, the same distant, preoccupied air. Max followed her out into the bright sunlight, loose-hipped and lazy. Nelson stood swishing flies in the near paddock. She felt happier. At least, when they all left, she would have Max and Nelson, she could romp with the dog freely, ride the horse whenever she wanted, out from under her father's eyes. It made her feel freer, just to think of it.

She threw a blanket and strap around Nelson, hitched herself up, and rode out along the dry creek until the land turned sharply upwards. She kept to the cool larches and the shadowed side of the rocks while she could, until the dry creek disappeared into shale. The horse swished along quietly, picking his way through the tangled scrub and the thorns of matagouri. When they got to the stream, she let Nelson drink, standing knee-high in the cool pebbled water. The sound of the stream was lulling; Alexa hung, mesmerised by the warmth and movement, between the present and her conversation with Tod in the shed. The early afternoon soothed her and she found she could think clearly about what had been said.

She knew there were rites of passage — the walkabout of the Australian boy, the first lion hunt of the young Masai, the first big sea journey of the Polynesian boy. It was the stuff books were written about, good books, full of adventure in places far away. She thought about how many of those stories she'd read, how she loved curling herself on her bed in winter, while the dark rain slashed against the window, with the book fat and warm in her hands. It had never bothered her, or even occurred to her, that they were all about boys . . . but now she remembered, and it did bother her. What had Tod meant, he was now a *man?* She knew he was trying to prove himself, to show that he had left his childhood behind him, but why was being a man a concept which suddenly, unfairly, excluded her? Was there to be, then, a time, a specific time, when she would become a woman? Would she know when that was? Her periods had begun; that was certainly nothing special, just inconvenient. It couldn't be that. Maybe it was babies — having babies. She shivered, remembering the baby, and how bony and clumsy she felt holding it. Max barked and the afternoon plummeted to the hot dusty present.

The stream had twisted and dropped ahead into a steep narrow gully. The ground was giving way to schist slides, not unmanageable but slow-going. Below her at the gully bottom, where the land was briefly swampy, a man was leading a limping horse. When he saw Alexa, he waved and called up to her. She saw that he had his free arm oddly cradled in his sleeve. She tethered Nelson to a tea tree and scrambled down the slope.

It was Clive, one of her father's hired musterers. It was clear the horse had slipped, perhaps on his way down the slope, lamed himself and thrown his rider.

'Bloody bad luck, eh,' he said to her, grinning ruefully. He examined the wrist thoughtfully; it hung limp and the skin was turning a mottled blue. He held out his arm to her, and she took his hand nervously. He grinned again.

'I can't fix it,' she mumbled, wanting to drop the warm hand. Why was he grinning at her like that? She felt her face get hot, and she dropped the hand, not caring if it hurt him.

'Thought you could tell if it was broke,' he said. He reached into his pocket, took out a crushed packet of cigarettes and tried to light one with one hand. She watched him sullenly; he expected her to help. He handed her the matchbox, and she opened it clumsily, taking out a match. The wind put out the flame almost immediately, and when she lit another, it too went out.

'You got to hold your hand around it — like this,' he said, in that easy voice. Alexa wanted to shout: don't touch me! but could not, and when she finally lit the cigarette, he puffed on it for a moment, looking up at the slide she'd just come down.

'Bloody horse,' he said, calmly. 'Reckon you'll have to help me up there — twisted my foot a bit, too.' Clive grinned at her again, and she felt as if she were squirming under the blue eyes that made her face grow hot again. He was a tall wiry man, hard, tanned, his hair bleached to the same brown colour as his face. He seemed more like an animal to Alexa, a horse perhaps, all brown with muscles. Would he feel like a horse, soft and hard at the same time? The feeling that hit the pit of her stomach suddenly, revulsion mixed with something unrecognisable, made her almost nauseous. She turned quickly, grabbing the reins of the man's horse, and started up the slope.

'Hey,' the man called. She turned around. He was still at the bottom, staring up at her.

'What,' she said, shortly. Inside she cried, no, no — you don't need any help! Climb the hill by yourself! But Clive really was helpless, unable to grasp scrub or balance himself enough to climb, and his twisted ankle made him wince. Alexa saw the wince. She slapped the rump of the horse, and it slowly climbed up to stand beside Nelson. Scrambling down, every move she made she was conscious of how clumsy she was, how red her face was, how the sweat made her shirt stick to her. Without a word, she slipped her shoulder under Clive's good arm, stood upright, and he leaned on her as she struggled back up the steep slope. He helped her as much as he could, and she felt his body pressing against her side, felt the long muscles of his arm and shoulder over her. The sudden feeling in the pit of her stomach had turned to a hard lump, but no longer made her sick. She hated this man, this stupid hired man who couldn't even ride properly. What was he doing, going mustering, if he was going to get thrown at the smallest gully? Then the thought flashed through her mind: if this man couldn't go, her father would be short-handed! He'd have to take her, for there wasn't time to find someone else! The idea elated her. The strength and agility returned to her legs and body, and the nearness of Clive no longer affected her. She decided she could be nice to this man, after all — what did it matter that he looked at her so strangely, in that way which made her flustered and angry at the same time? Who cared? Because of him, she could go!

At the ridge-top, she stopped to catch her breath. The man didn't let go of her for a second, but stood looking down into her face. Impatiently, she waited, feeling him breathing hard in pain and exhaustion. Let's go, she said to herself impatiently. She wanted to get back, to hear her father say he needed her to go. Her face must have been happy, for Clive smiled at her.

'Thanks, love,' he said. She helped him on Nelson, and though it took almost an hour to walk slowly home, they didn't speak. Once she looked back at him, and she saw him staring at her as if he wanted to speak. She opened her mouth but didn't know what to say. In embarrassment, they looked at each other, until Alexa turned back to lead the horse. The feeling in her stomach churned up again.

Jim received Clive with concern, as much because of his hurt as because it meant he would be short a man and a horse. They sat at the kitchen table, Marty fixing a pot of tea and Jim wrapping the swollen wrist. Alexa hung near the door, eager, embarrassed, waiting for the word from her father. Of course, he'd need her help now! It was clear he would. The tea boiled.

'Lucky your girl came along, eh,' said Clive to Jim. 'Would have been stuck there all night, hadn't been for her.' He looked back at her and smiled. Her insides twisted up; she knew he looked at her the way the boys on the benches in town looked at girls walking past. She found herself edging closer to the table, telling herself she wanted to catch Jim's attention. But she could also study Clive better from her new position.

'I'll take you in to the doctor in about an hour,' said Jim. 'I don't think it's broken, but I reckon you won't be able to muster. Know any bloke I could ask? — I'll be short without you.'

Alexa caught her breath. Now! Now he would turn, see her; now he would realise what he'd just overlooked before. She leaned towards him, eager, forgetting Clive. Jim looked at her, absently.

'Oh, Lexa, we'll have to use Nelson now — I need another horse. Take him over to Bob to have him shod, will you?'

Even then, it didn't hit her, not for a split moment. When it did, the kitchen seemed to go black. She saw Clive, Jim, her mother, through a haze. She was not to go, no matter what. It didn't even occur to her to ask straight out. The shame would be too much, in front of Clive . . .

Marty saw the blankness pass over her daughter's face, felt the emptiness. Inside, she cried out for her. She wondered when it was that she herself had stopped wishing to ride off with Jim, or with her father before that, to have adventures. Jim turned to her, his face puzzled, questioning. Alexa flung herself from the room, stumbled over the door-frame, slammed the screen.

'What'd I say?' he asked Marty.

'Oh, Jim. She wants to *go* with you! She wants to go on the muster — didn't you know that?' She told him, knowing it wouldn't matter, knowing he couldn't change his way of thinking.

'Muster's no place for a girl!' laughed Clive. 'All kinds of rough stuff up there, eh.' Jim nodded, looking towards the door, confused. He hadn't even known — but how could she think she'd be able to go? What could he do for her, to make it up? He looked again at Marty, but her face was closed, hard, and she turned away from the two men.

Outside the door, Alexa leaned against the cool boards of the house. She couldn't move, so strong was the desire to destroy something. She couldn't move with an odd fear, with a burning shame. Her side ached where Clive's body had pressed against it up the slope; she felt again the hardness of his ribs, his muscles. It made her writhe inside, until her hands jerked convulsively. She felt the weight of a great betrayal, by Jim, by her mother, by herself, her own body that could not seem to act normally when that musterer sat at their table.

She was of no use to anyone; she belonged nowhere. Her clothes felt tight on her; she tugged at them ferociously. Max crept under a woodpile, and lay silently, crushed.

She wished Clive could die from a broken wrist. She was willing to wait patiently for his death. If only she'd never seen him in the gully. It was his fault. She felt shamed. She ran to Nelson, convulsively brushed his back with a curry comb. She scraped at him, needing to remove any trace of that man who'd ridden him. Even Nelson was not hers, now. Jim had taken him, as casually and easily as he could take anything, Max, her dreams. There was nothing for her.

The horse pushed at her with his warm nose. His eye, deep, purple-brown, bright and dark, stared at her. It was an eye like the eye of an old Maori, like Billy Turoa's eye, as if it contained all the peace and knowledge in the world. Billy. Billy. She saw his old seamed face clearly, heard his flat strong voice. *One day, I saw him . . .* and the story unfolded itself inside her, filled her, gave steadiness to her whirling

30

self. She stood straight, led Nelson to the blacksmith's truck and tethered him.

There *were* things Jim could not take from her. Things that were secret. Stories. Her drawings. Writing — she could write what she wanted. No one could take that. Stories could never leave her: Billy had said that once. He couldn't take the pictures of otters away from inside her head, and now she allowed herself to look at them, swimming, powerful, lithe and strong, in a dark hidden lake. They raised their sleek broad heads, looked at her from those same dark brown eyes, inviting her — to what? To find them?

She found she had wandered past the house and was leaning against the cool, acrid-smelling corrugation of a tin shed. The tin rasped on her skin and felt so good against her heated face. The voices she heard through the wall grasped her attention and she listened. She could hear Clive's voice. The men were helping him pack to go into town.

'Yeah, she's a strange one — wanted to go on the muster!' he said. There was a muffled chuckle from another man.

'What'd you do for an hour with her in the bush, eh, Clive!' came a voice, ribbing the other man.

'Don't be barmy — she's a kid!' said Clive. The men inside laughed again. There was the sound of boots hitting the floor, the squeak of a bunk.

'Not much, she's a kid! Seems like no time, since they was kids, her an' Tod. But look at Tod, all grown up — and that girl, she's no kid!'

'She'll be a funny looker, though, eh. Can't tell how pretty. Bet she likes you, Clive! Take her out when you get back!'

There was the sound of an embarrassed grunt from Clive, and more chuckles from the men. Alexa stood frozen against the outside wall. She couldn't believe she was hearing this.

'Well, I *do* like her. She's no goose; she's got a lot of sense. I bet she wouldn't be half bad on a muster, eh!' came this final shot from Clive, defensive. The shed door opened on the other side. Alexa couldn't move. She saw Clive's wrist all bandaged up. She wanted to touch it. She wanted to rip at it, tear off the whole wrist and throw it all blue and horrible on the floor. She wanted to hold his arm, she wanted to feel the smooth brown skin . . . She hated him, she hated the whole world, she wanted to hear him say he liked her again. The tin wall of the shed dug into her, the bolts pressing painfully into her.

'You bloody bastards! You bloody, bloody awful bastards!' she cried after the men. But they were across the yard now; they didn't hear her. Thank God everyone was gone. No one would see her crying.

3

HER ROOM, AS always, was like a small dark cave, safe and shut against the world. Alexa leaned her elbows on the desk top. The hurt and rage of the day before had dimmed somewhat, but she felt bruised and needed to be alone. She had avoided eating breakfast when her father and the other men were in the kitchen, but later she'd run down, and Marty had kept her plate warm and allowed her to take it to her room. Alexa looked for an excuse to stay in the kitchen, wanting to be near Marty, but afraid Jim or Tod would come in, she fled to her room.

Now, her breakfast finished, she pushed the plate aside and began again what she had started earlier that morning, her school term paper. On the top of the first page, in large letters, was the word KEA. Underneath, neatly, she printed: *An Endangered Bird of the South Island.* She sighed and re-read the paragraph she'd written. How much could be said about those great noisy parrots? It was certainly hard to imagine them endangered. An hour's ride or less in any direction would take one into kea country where the green alpine birds rooted in the tussock, snipped the heads from mountain daisies, stripped bright snowberries from their branches. The birds would rise with a clatter and screeches at a rider's approach, the sun glinting on their olive-green backs and blazing off the startling orange and yellow of their under-wings. The farmers killed them, although they were protected. Nothing could convince them they didn't kill sheep. Hadn't they seen the cheeky birds crawling on the still-moving carcass of a lamb, pecking the eyes from the still-breathing ewe?

She ran the pen up and down her cheek, sat, idly drew a sinuous form in the margin of the page. The form grew, took on shape, became a beast with sleek body and broad head, became large-eyed and swimming, became the otter. She looked at it.

'This is daft,' she said aloud. 'I don't want to write about those stupid birds!' She crumpled the paper up and threw it in the corner, pushed back her chair and went to stare out the window.

Tod was brushing dried mud off his horse, Bing, in the yard. Beyond him, a man leaned against a shed and smoked, on his tea break. He reminded her of Clive; in fact, all the men had that same hard, easy-boned walk, the same brown body and brown face from wind and sun. She felt again the stab in her gut that both compelled her to watch and yet repelled her. In the small holding-yard, Nelson stood, newly-shod, dozing in the sun. How could she bear to have one of those big men on his back? How could she bear to ride him, knowing that for more than a week, his sides would be clasped by those long hard legs, those striding, *foreign* muscles? She shuddered. Tod! She'd ask Tod. She didn't mind Tod riding Nelson.

The kennelled dogs set up a chorus of barking that always accompanied the sound of a truck rattling up the metal road. She peered past the yard through the dark ring of macrocarpa trees. A blue pick-up coughed through the gate and jerked to a stop, covered with dun-dry dust. In the back was a mound of leather, an ancient saddle and old blankets. A small mottled-blue dog balanced itself on the roof of the cab.

Billy! she cried to herself, then: 'Billy! Billy Turoa!' she called through the window glass. She clattered down the stairs and burst through the door to greet the wiry old man she'd known her whole life. He always showed up at the station in this way. He never missed a shearing season that

Alexa could remember, but she didn't remember him ever coming at mustering; as always, his visits were unexplained and welcomed. No one at the station knew where he'd come from or where he went when he left. Every Maori she'd met had strong family ties, came from a *marae* which was the centre of their social and religious life. But Billy never spoke of family, *marae,* or place. Sometimes Alexa imagined that her father knew, and kept Billy's secret.

He looked very old, this time. He seemed to have a limp she hadn't noticed before. But he still smiled at her with that familiar, dignified smile, shook her hand as he shook her father's. As always, too, she suddenly felt honoured, special, and everything around her seemed sharply in focus.

He greeted Marty quietly, with warmth and respect. He rarely touched people, and said little, but his face expressed everything. He had not seen the new baby, and held her carefully when Marty held her out to him. Alexa watched, strangely shy. Inside herself, she was singing. He knew, he *knew!* she cried joyfully, feeling it bursting against her chest. I needed him to come! How did he *know*? She could feel her mouth smiling and she relaxed it, wanting to be all contained within herself, so no one could see.

It did not occur to her that she hadn't thought in terms of *seeing* Billy, before. But now, at his arrival, it was as if she'd been wanting to see him, talk with him, for weeks. The very first chance she got, she'd ask him to tell her the story. She'd hear the words: 'One day, I saw him.' Had she remembered the story right? It was so long since Billy was last here — perhaps she'd forgotten some vital part! She could feel warmth stealing through her, as if she'd been cold; it was like being hugged from inside, this anticipation of *her* story.

Billy sat at the kitchen table slurping thoughtfully at his tea, running it around his mouth as if it were some new and exotic taste. He drank three cups in this way. Alexa watched him, entranced. Her tea, also, tasted new and wonderful. Tod sat opposite, watching also.

'I reckon it's a good thing you came along,' said Jim. 'I lost a bloke yesterday — wrist broke. We're all set to go tomorrow

35

— will you ride with me?' Billy nodded, and Jim leaned back in the chair. It was all settled. He looked at his son and daughter, saw them watching Billy, felt happy. More than anyone else, Jim trusted Billy.

Billy and Jim went outside to look at the horses, and pick out one for Billy to ride. Billy always carried his saddle in the back of the truck, but Alexa had never known him to have a horse. She was reminded again with a small pang that Nelson would be going, too, ridden by some strange sweaty man. She squirmed. When she rode Nelson, it was as if they were one creature. She pictured one of the men on his back, felt her face grow hot, hugged her arms about herself. She looked for Tod through the house.

He was in the tiny cluttered room Jim used for a study. It had an old leather chair which rocked back alarmingly when it was sat in, but it never toppled. Tod was sprawled in it with a map spread out over his lap; he squinted in the poor light. His fingers traced the routes they'd take during the next several days while he studied the beats. The first took them over the low range of Robin's Pass, down the steep gorge beyond, and out on to the flat along the river. It was a good place to hold a mob of sheep, with good tussock, and a hut for the men. He felt warm and giddy-strong. It would be the first time he'd stay in that hut as a real musterer. He leaned back in the chair, running his finger over the map lovingly.

'Will you ride Nelson?'

Tod jumped; he hadn't heard her approach. In the dim light of the hallway, lit only by the small yellow lamp, her face was almost all shadow. It made her look smaller. Her hair, face and clothes were all the same warm blond-browny colour. Her hands hung loosely at her sides. Why should she want him to ride Nelson? He knew he was being trusted with something, and he hesitated, not wanting to say the wrong thing.

'Sure I will,' he answered finally, softly. His voice surprised them both. Her hands came together in front of her, and the shadows broke apart on her face; she smiled. Tod smoothed the map on his knees, looking down at it.

'And I'll look after him really carefully, put a blanket on him at night. Don't worry. He's good, got good feet. I'll check them every night.' He felt his whole chest expanding, as if he were too big for his clothes. What had he done? He wasn't sure, he only felt that smile in the lamp-light; he'd said something right.

In sudden panic, Alexa said: 'But what about Bing? You'd rather ride Bing!' Bing had been given to him on his twelfth birthday, a yearling, boy and colt together.

'Billy needs a good horse; he can ride Bing. That way, I can sort of watch after them both, you know?'

Alexa squeezed her hands together, suspicious. Wasn't he being unusually generous and understanding? She peered at him in the dark study. His face was honest, beyond suspicion.

'Thank you,' she said. They were both surprised and startled again, like puppies when they discover they can bark. It was funny, a funny sensation, talking like this, like adults. No squabbling.

'I just — I just didn't want one of those guys on my horse . . .'

'What's wrong with them? They're okay,' said Tod.

'Oh, I know. I know that. They're just awfully big. They're . . . well, Nelson isn't used to strangers, that's all!'

Well, he could understand that. She was right. A horse is valuable. It has to be treated well. He smiled at her. Somehow, he wasn't sure how, he'd done something for her that was so important it had made her tongue-tied. He rattled the map.

'Want to see where we're going?' he asked. She came into the study now.

'First, we got to muster them out of here, clean up this gully, see . . . Then we hold them here for the night.' He looked at her with shining eyes.

'Billy says it might snow!' Snow was not the enemy to him that it was to the older men, not the death and hard work raking freezing paths through to sheep, digging them out from ice-encrusted holes.

37

'He said he can smell it at night!' He watched Alexa studying the map.

'What does that mean?' she asked, pointing to the uneven, concentric lines.

'That shows the land — you know, the hills, how high they are, and gullies and spurs, there. See this number, that's metres, how high the hill is. So you can figure out the easy way to go.'

'Where's this?' she pointed to the far upper corner of the map. She could see the little mark of their homestead. It was almost diagonally opposite to where she now looked.

'I don't know. Not us, I reckon. Maybe leased land. Here, let me see . . .' He grabbed the map and held it closer to the light. The concentric circles were more erratic up towards that corner. They were intersected by hundreds of tiny rivers and streams, and very few place-names. There was a tiny, perfectly oval lake, and the numbers around it, indicating the height of the moutains, were very high. She had her finger near it, and stared at it, fascinated. It was a jewel, so perfect, a drop of turquoise. She moved her finger towards it, almost dazed. Billy, here . . . a man alone on a horse, and a lake hidden in the mountains . . . so perfect . . . just the place to see an otter. . .

'Well, it's nothing to do with us, I reckon,' said Tod, folding up the map. 'There's lots of places no one's been. Only wild sheep, eh. Too rough.' He stuffed the map into the top drawer of the desk, and she watched where it went.

Alexa pounded up the stairs to her room and sat, breathless, at her desk. It was all a sign, everything! The building-up of problems, Billy coming, the map . . . Why hadn't she thought of that before! It was Billy's coming, she knew. Who needed to go on the muster? She had her own search! Oh, if I could just leave, *leave!*' she whispered fiercely, pushing her papers into a loose pile. 'I know I could find the otter, I know it! I *know* he's out there.'

It was then, in the dark calm of her room, she decided to search for the otter of Billy's stories. The restlessness, boredom, the anger at Jim, at Tod, that terrible, fascinating stab in her stomach when she thought of Clive — it all disintegrated with the sudden flash of decision. Yes. She would go, ride out on whatever horse was left, take Max, and go. She wanted to be totally alone, away from her father's judgements, Marty's kitchen, the baby, away from the boredom of school assignments and endless chores.

'If I could just *do* something!' she whispered again, urgently. She got up, rummaged through her drawers. What to take? She couldn't sit still now the decision was so clear. She fidgeted, sat down again. Outside, she heard the motor of a truck revving up. It was an old motor — Billy's truck. She ran to the window. Billy was in the cab, jiggling the ignition key.

'Wait! Billy! Wait!' She flew down the stairs. Marty looked startled as she banged into the kitchen.

'Where's Billy going? Is he going to town? I'm going, okay? I'm going with him . . .' She grabbed her jersey off a hook and slammed the door behind her. Marty sighed and took a pot off the stove. She heard the old motor catch, the engine start and looking out of the window, saw Alexa clamber into the cab, settle on the cracked vinyl seat with the foam coming out. The dust rose in the sunlight as Billy bumped the truck down the road.

They sat comfortably silent for quite a while. The old truck made such a din on the metal road that no conversation would be easy, anyway. The dust seeped into the cab, settling on their clothes. Although she could not see him, Alexa knew the blue collie rode the cab-top above her, with perfect balance.

She didn't get to town often. When she and Tod were younger, still in primary school, Marty had driven them the six kilometres to the main road to catch the schoolbus every morning. She remembered those daily drives through the lower blocks of the station. It had seemed greener then, and there hadn't been as many rabbits. The land now was dun and brown, stricken with drought and over-grazing; it was a poor station, rugged, poorly grassed, overrun with rabbits. The main road running by theirs was in as bad a condition as the metal one, the hardtop broken and uneven. But the town had grown. The train stopped there now, several times a day, and you could go to Nelson, or south to Christchurch, where Tod had gone to school.

Going to town always reminded her of school, of going away from the station. Her mother wanted her to go, as Tod had gone, instead of studying alone by correspondence. She felt a stab of sympathy for Tod. He'd gone for more than two years, coming home only during summer holidays and breaks. She had a sudden revelation about Tod going on the muster. It must be for him like the shedding of a restricting skin, the uniform, the rules, the strangers, the musty smells of chalk and old wood floors, the lack of space, of air itself. How could she resent him, knowing that? She'd gone, for a week once, to 'try it out', as her mother said. It strangled her even now, to remember. The din, the echoes, the tiny green bedrooms, the classes in the gymnasium full of eager, sweaty girls yelling lustily, pounding the floors like young summer calves. Classes in French with that awful Miss Lamont . . .

The truck rattled to a stop at the railway crossing, and they waited while the red cars of the train whooshed by. She'd been lost in thought longer than she'd imagined, for the railway was barely two kilometres from town. She sat up, eager. Billy smiled across at her. How wonderful that he never asked her silly things, like now, like why was she going to town with him? She wouldn't have known the answer.

They pulled up behind Woolworths. Billy took a crumpled list from his pocket and read it aloud to her.

'Number eight wire, one coil. Six tin plates. Needle and thread . . .' He grinned at her. 'That's for me. Never get through a job without rippin' something. Oilskin — that's me, too. Come for a visit, your dad puts me to work. Oatmeal. Sugar. Boot nails.' He pulled out his wallet and studied its contents. 'Reckon I can afford all that — luxuries, eh!' Alexa grinned back.

They went into the hardware store first. Billy bought much more than was on his list: pliers, wire snippers, and a small trowel. Alexa wondered what it was for. She stared out on the street. It was quiet, not many people about. She wanted to talk to Billy before they went home.

'Do you want a pie?' she asked him, after a while.

'I want to get this stuff in the truck first. You go, I'll meet you in there,' he said, stuffing his purchases in a bag. He hung the roll of wire over his shoulder and walked back to the truck. Alexa turned down the street to the takeaway bar.

The door of the place opened as she came nearer, and her stomach plummeted violently. Clive walked out, carrying a bag dark with grease stains. When he saw her, he called to her. His wrist was bandaged heavily, and he walked with a limp. Here on the footpath, in town, no longer in his natural element of wind and sky and tussock, he seemed younger even, shyer. She saw he couldn't be older than twenty. She didn't know what to say, and stood miserably as he approached.

'G'day!' he said, happily. 'Quite a mess I got in, eh!' He held out his wounded wrist to her, as he had in the gully. She examined it stupidly, the shame of the day before welling inside her. She tried to see his face without him noticing. He didn't seem ill at ease.

'What're you going to do now?' she asked at last, for something to say.

'Oh, I signed up for the dole this morning, first thing,' he said. 'Beats dishwashin', eh. Only kind of job I'm cut for is out there . . .' and he gestured vaguely in the direction of the hills. He smiled down at her, liking her plain, tanned face, the straight blond-brown hair. She was tall and strong-looking, and he remembered seeing her on the horse, from the bottom of the gully. She'd seemed a part of the animal. He didn't know many men who could ride so naturally.

'Reckon I'll stay the winter here — doctor figures the wrist'll be fine by lambin'. Your dad have work at lambin'?'

'I don't know,' she replied, shortly. She liked what he'd said about his work, where he could work. She knew what he meant. She could not imagine being anywhere other than in those jagged hills, the gullies and valley choked with scrub and tussock, with hawks wheeling above her in the wind. For a second, reckless, she thought she might tell *him* about her plan, her wild plan to look for the otter. She examined his face, open, simple, handsome. She felt more at ease, but knew he was not the person to tell. Only Billy could know.

41

'Well,' he said, slowly, not knowing what else to say to her. He couldn't remember how old she was supposed to be, but he figured it was too young to ask her out. She had no expression in her voice, and certainly didn't giggle like most girls . . .

Alexa started in the store. 'I have to go now,' she said. She saw Billy coming back from the truck.

'We're getting pies,' she added, feeling idiotic again, her face hot once more. Why was he just standing there?

'Oh,' he answered. He turned away, then back again, suddenly.

'You like the pictures?' he asked abruptly.

'I guess so.'

'You reckon you'd like to go sometime?'

'Sure, I guess so,' she said in a strangled voice, and ran into the store. Now why had she said that? What a stupid thing to say. She ordered meat pies and Cokes for Billy and herself, and sat at the cracked formica-topped table, disconsolate. She felt a rush of fear. What if he phoned her tonight, or tomorrow? She hadn't decided when she was leaving yet, but suddenly she knew it had to be tomorrow or the next day. She propped her head in her hands in anguish. If he called her tomorrow, what could she say? She had to look for the otter. She had to. But if he didn't call then, he might call later in the week — and she wouldn't be there. Maybe he'd give up on her then.

Billy's presence calmed her. The meat pies steamed in their hands, too hot to eat. They broke them open on the plates and let them cool.

'Tell me about the otter, Billy?' she asked quietly, at last. She had wanted to talk to him all day.

'How can I tell you that story without you sittin' on my knee?' he answered her. She was stung. She ignored his grin. He began to eat his pie, biting in great steaming mouthfuls. She poked at hers; it was still too hot.

'I'm not a little girl any more, Billy!' she cried, trying to maintain her dignity. Was it possible he was laughing at her? Billy? 'I don't want just a nice story. I need to know this stuff! I need to know what you saw! It's not just a story, is it?'

42

and she knew there was pleading in her voice.

'You know I saw an otter, Alexa,' said Billy, suddenly serious, and his deep black eyes pierced her with the swiftness of a tiny lizard running from shadow to light.

She felt ashamed of her mistrust.

'The story is yours,' he said at last. 'The otter, *seeing* the otter, that's mine. It's always that way. What you see is yours. When you tell it to someone else, it is a story then, and it is theirs.' He stared at her with eyes now flat and implacable.

'No, you aren't a little girl, no more. But I didn't ever tell you that story 'cause you were a little kid. I told you 'cause you *wanted to hear it.*' He drew his big rough hand across his mouth. He had a wide, broad mouth, sensuous, like a younger man's. It smiled at her now, just a bit.

'You're going to look for the otter.' It wasn't a question, but a statement. She wasn't surprised. It was all part of it, all part of what she had to do, that Billy would know, too. She thought of Clive for a moment, thinking how she'd almost told him in her desire to let it out. Billy, too, was like Clive, a man, not just a story-teller, not just a comfortable lap to sit on begging for stories. He had his own secrets, wishes. She wondered if he'd ever married.

He pulled a bag out from under the table where he'd propped it while he ate. He shoved it across to her.

'Present,' he said. She made a small sound of surprise, tore at the bag. Inside was a small fat pad of drawing paper bound with a spiral holder, and two soft black pencils. There was also a smaller, soft parcel wrapped in another bag and taped. She opened it more slowly. Inside was a bright red scarf, made of some filmy, light material that slid through her hand with a faint whisper. Her eyes glowed. She had never had a gift from Billy. How had he known she did drawings? She'd never shown anyone. She felt the paper. It was fine and thick, pebbled like a fine book.

'So you can draw my otter,' he grinned at her, and once again, she did not know if he laughed at her or at himself. She held the red scarf against her cheek.

'It's for when you want the world to see you,' he said. 'It's for when you want to walk out and say "Here I am!"' He fingered the red material in Alexa's hand. 'Maybe you'll wear it when you go out with Clive!'

At last she managed to gasp, 'How did you know that?' Her face felt on fire. He got up and paid the bill, laughing down at her.

'Well, I saw him, didn't I? I saw him lookin' at you. I'm old but I ain't daft!'

She gathered the gifts and held them against her. They were treasures. She'd take them with her. She would draw his otter, *her* otter. She'd draw it; she'd write about it . . . she'd write that silly paper for science about the otter, and the silly teacher would not know what to say.

'Thank you,' she said finally. 'Thank you.'

4

IT WAS A grand parade when the men left the next morning. The four men, Tod, her father, and Billy, and after them the packhorses strung out like loose beads on a chain. Milling about the points on this slow-moving thread were the fifteen or so dogs, eager and tense. Everything was infused with the same deep dun-colour, the same rough animal-browns: the horses, saddles, sacks and men, the dogs with their mottled brown coats, blankets rolled behind saddles, the ground, the sky, all seeming to blend with the tone of an old photograph — dun-gold, slow and dignified. When they were barely ten minutes away, at the far end of the home paddock, they were indistinguishable from the earth, except by movement. But what an assembly! It was the strongest horse, the toughest man, the quickest dog, off to the wild mountains and sky.

Alexa allowed herself the romantic vision of herself as a damsel waving her knight off to battle. She waved the red scarf Billy had given her in lazy, fluttering loops over her head. The vision lasted less than a minute; the dull ache returned, the restlessness intruded, making her stomach jolt and her hand drop, the scarf limp at her side. She was no damsel! It was *she* who was the knight, *she* who had a quest; she would be the poor knight, without horse or armour, and go off into the unknown in search of her dream. This image pleased her and she wound the scarf around her neck and tied it in a dashing knot.

Against the hill, the procession moved even slower. Tod gripped Nelson's sides in excitement. They were on their way! The horses laboured up the steep slope, the dogs wove nervously in and out, the men called to each other. It was barely dawn, but as he looked back towards the homestead, he saw the tiny figure of his sister standing and watching. He caught sight of the movement of the red scarf, saw it wave, drop, and then saw it fastened around her neck. He wanted to laugh. The weird things she did!

He cantered up to Jim.

'Thanks for lettin' me ride Nelson,' he said. Jim's face had become relaxed, now the muster was actually under way. It creased into a smile, hearing this.

'She liked that, did she?' He paused, then: 'Take special care of him — sure hate taking him like that, eh. She never even said goodbye . . .'

'I don't know, Dad. Look, she's still watching us!' Jim turned, saw the small figure standing by the gate. Marty had gone into the house to begin her long day. He grinned.

'I'll be damned,' he said softly, pleased. He raised his hand once, without looking back. Why was it always so hard, leaving the women? he mused, thinking of Marty. So like Alexa, she'd been, when he'd first met her. But *she'd* never wanted to go mustering, or anything like that . . .

'Why didn't you want Lexa, Dad?' asked Tod suddenly. The question threw him. His son stared up at him. 'She sure does ride as good as me, eh. She was really good the time those sheep broke out when we were dippin' them —'

The question hung there, something resented. Jim studied the mountains ahead of him. He was here, this was *his* place; he was alone with rock and sky and wind. The other men were as much a part of the landscape as the tea tree and the hawks. The idea of women intruded: that was all emotion, talk, questions, babies, softness . . .

'Well, look Tod: isn't this good, eh? Out here, just us? Just you and your mates? Wait'll you hear them talking tonight! Couldn't talk like that with your mum along, eh!' He spoke lightly. Tod's face broke into a pleased grin.

'No, guess not,' he said happily, settling comfortably on Nelson's back.

'We don't stick to any posh behaviour, out there,' continued Jim. 'Eat out of tins, eh, sit around stinkin' after a good day...! Couldn't really do that with Lexa around!' They laughed together, as if they'd made a pact against the thing which disturbed them both. Tod sat up in the saddle. He *did* feel freer, suddenly loosed from restraints, confusions, speech. No need for talk here, except to swear from excess energy, jovially, or to tell a coarse joke, a dog story, to laugh. He sighed happily, home forgotten.

The chain of men, horses and dogs topped the far hills and disappeared from sight. Alexa turned towards the house. Just her, her mother, the baby — she felt an intense weight had fallen from her back. No one to watch them! No one to glance at her as she sat idly on a fence for hours, staring into the mountains. She untied Max, let him bound free, to course through the yard. It was so good, it was *good* to break the rules!

The dog nudged at the door into the kitchen. The fat baby screamed in delight, kicking her legs as if she, too, felt the sudden lifting of constraints. Marty pursed her lips, looking down at the big dog and her daughter flushed and excited.

'Mum! Let's go on a picnic! C'mon!' cried Alexa, and the great dog wiggled in front of the woman expectantly. Marty's face softened into a smile, feeling an absurd temptation to giggle. No dog was ever allowed into the house, certainly not Max. She revelled in the luxury of the animal.

'Well, I reckon we have the place all to ourselves today!' she laughed. 'What are we going to do with *you*, you useless mutt!' she laughed, rubbing his ears. Alexa sat next to Max. How warm her mother was. Everyone loved her, even the rough hired men. She was so tall, and strong, and so soft to touch. Alexa leaned against her leg for a moment.

'Mum, would Dad really shoot Max?' she asked, in the space of that quick closeness. Her mother could take away a fear, like she took away sickness and hurt when she was a little girl.

'You know what he things about things not pulling their weight . . .'

'I know what *he* thinks! I want to know what *you* think!'

Marty, startled, stared down at her daughter. Such a solemn, intense face — she caught her breath. It could have been herself, staring back from a mirror, twenty years ago. But there was something . . . something different . . . it wouldn't have been her, really. Why did she look so deeply at everything? Why couldn't she just worry about boys, clothes, going out — like other girls? Marty sighed. She'd already met Jim by the time she was Alexa's age.

'*I* think it's enough that you love the dog,' she said finally.

'You mean, you mean you reckon it's all right I have him? You don't think he's useless?' Alexa stood up eagerly. Maybe her mother understood; maybe she *was* on her side.

'Well, you know he's useless, Lexa, but I think he's fine and I think you should keep him.' Marty said all this in a rush, feeling as if she were betraying her husband. She almost wished she hadn't spoken, seeing the look of hope on Alexa's face.

'Oh, Mum!' cried Alexa, feeling the surge of love like a huge warm substance covering her inside and out. The words spilled from her. Maybe, after all, her mother would know how to dispel her fears and restlessness.

'Why does Dad have to have a use for everything? Can't things just *be,* sometimes? He just shoots anything he can't use!' She sat hard down on the floor next to the dog. Marty picked up the baby, burying her face in the soft skin. What could she say? Her mind raced — questions, questions. Wasn't there anything she could tell, *give,* her daughter?

'What about people, Mum? Like me! What about me? I reckon I'm not much use, eh!' The intensity of the girl's voice prodded Marty to speak.

'People are different, Lexa. You know that!' She opened her shirt and began to feed the baby. Alexa looked away, suddenly nervous. Her stomach contracted. Her mother did not, could not, feel like she did. She knew it surely. The baby was what did it; there was a *reason* for her mother, and it

48

satisfied her completely. She didn't want to go out with the men into the mountains, hunting sheep. She didn't wonder about what lay beyond those mountains, or anything as wild and far-fetched as the idea of otters living in some hidden lake . . . The baby suckled softly, and the sound curled the corners of Marty's mouth. I couldn't, thought Alexa; I just *couldn't* . . . do that. Have babies and that's it!

'Oh, Lexa!' said Marty at last. 'There *is* a use for you. There is a place for you. But I don't know what it is. When I was your age . . .' She paused, looking back.

'When you were my age — what?' asked Alexa impatiently.

'Well, I just wasn't so. . . I don't know. I liked to sew, and I liked going to town for ice-cream with the other girls, and meeting the boys there. That's how I met your dad!'

'Didn't you ever want to *do* something?' cried Alexa. She hated this picture of her mother; it angered her.

'I did, Lexa,' said Marty, her voice strong. 'People are different, and what they want for themselves is different. I don't *know* what you want. I knew what *I* wanted, and maybe that makes me lucky. It wasn't a big thing, just a home, your father, my children — you. I wanted you. It was what I wanted to do.' Marty was surprised at the sharpness in her voice. Alexa's expression challenged her. She struggled to see the way her daughter did, to feel the struggles, the frustrations, the nameless wants she knew the girl lived with every day. Why was that so hard? She looked down at the brown smooth face. Was it a pretty face? She couldn't tell. Billy had told her they'd seen Clive in town. Clive was a good boy. He'd have his own station some day. She frowned; there was nothing she could say to help.

'I won't let your dad get rid of Max,' she said at last, slowly. It was the least she could do. 'You just go on with him the way you are. You've got him trained really well . . . keep him out from under foot. You'll just have to put up with Dad's complaints once in a while, but you have to accept he's got his ideas and his own ways. He's not going to sneak out and kill him, don't worry! Don't bring it up, and he won't feel he's got to do it so as not to lose face, that's all.'

It was a poor resolution. Alexa stared down at the floor. It seemed, poor as it was, the only solution. The weakness of it frightened her, but she knew Marty was right. Her father would not just take the dog and shoot it. But he would go on flaring up periodically if he were reminded of the dog and the best thing to do was not let him become reminded. She pulled herself up off the floor.

She took Max with her up to her room, half-expecting to be forbidden by her mother. But nothing was said. Max lay on the rug, and Alexa sat glumly at her desk.

It was always there, that same question, the one that always caused an unendurable restlessness to jerk through her body. She drummed her fingers on the desk-top. What *did* she want? Where was the right place for her? Already, she could admit that it was not to be a farmer, a sheep farmer on a dry windy station, like Tod would be. And it wasn't to be, like her mother, a farmer's wife! She knew everything she *didn't* want — especially not babies! I'm no fool, she thought fiercely. They're nothing special, even though everyone acts as though they are. Anyone can have babies! They all look alike, too! Everyone in the world had babies.

She carefully arranged the books and papers on her desk, making neat piles, categorising them. She looked around her tiny room comfortably. Everything had a place, the books, clothes, the bits of rock and wood from the beach, the mica stones found in the river, the woven horse-hair bracelet, the photos of Max, the carved lizard given to her once on holiday by an old Maori woman. She picked up the tiny carving, feeling the rough cuts in the wood. It was the sort of thing you could pick up in a tourist shop, but it seemed too old for that, a little cracked. She stared out at the grey afternoon. It looked cold and wet. The shed roofs glistened with a heavy mist. She thought of Tod out in the hills.

Would she really go out there, too? The otter was there, in some cold lake, that little jewel of a lake in the far corner of the map. The reality of the search hit her. How would she get there? The only horse left on the station that she could ride was Hobo, the old draft that had been her father's first horse.

Where would she sleep? Could she follow the map? What food could she take that would not arouse her mother's suspicions? The questions scared her so she shut them from her mind. She would go, that was all! She'd figure out the details as she went.

Alexa sat there a long time. Outside, the day darkened into an early drizzly evening. Her pencil fiddled on the paper in front of her. Drawings of something half-represented covered the margins. She wrote phrases down, fastened them together dreamily.

'My thoughts are clothed in otter skins,' she wrote, '... that flash and dive among dark weeds; through the darkest mountain lakes, they bring me tiny, perfect fish.'

She said them aloud in a sort of chant, pleased with the sound, and rearranged the words so they resembled a poem. She wrote more.

'I have heard the old man's tale. He said the otter looked at him, and would not let him go . . .' She surveyed the last bit critically. How could she write about these things? She hadn't even seen the otter, *any* otter at all, for that matter! She paced the room, fidgeting. Her old rucksack lay crumpled on a chair; she picked it up, shook it, testing out how much space was in it. From the kitchen, Marty was calling her.

A hundred jobs needed doing. The baby was fed and put in her cot. The dinner steamed on the stove. Alexa called the chooks, fed them and shut them up for the night. As usual, the rooster had to be chased and caught; he raked at her with his spurs and she angrily thrust him into the hen house. Four cows had gathered at the paddock gate, lowing. She led them swaying and chewing softly into the milking shed, where the yellow light of one light bulb steamed softly on their rain-dark hides.

Alexa and Marty sterilised the cups and fastened them on to two of the cows. The evening had become quickly cold and the rain had cleared. In the frosty air, the milk warmed the cold steel and moisture condensed on the metal. Mother and daughter stood quietly for a while, each by the head of a jersey, hearing the dull ping of milk inside the cannisters and the low purr of the milking machine's motor. The beautiful violet eyes of the cows blinked in the light, and they swung their heads, mashing cud. Outside the open shed, bright blue pukekos screamed in the low land near the wool sheds. It was so peaceful. The dark filled Alexa and her mother; the stars began to show, and the golden light banding the dark yard from the kitchen windows was warm and promising. In the quiet of the milking shed, hidden behind the huge head of the cow, Alexa ventured another question.

'Mum, when did you first realise you were becoming a woman? I mean, when do you think you stopped being a girl?'

Marty checked the suction on the cups attached to the cow's teats.

'Well, I guess there must have been a time when I stopped thinking of myself as a girl, but I don't think it was any special time. I don't know. Why?'

'Would you think I was a woman?' Alexa did not look at her mother as she asked this question. The shadows around the cows were large and sheltering, and it was almost as if her voice were not her own.

'You're still only fourteen, Lexa! *I* don't know ... in some ways, you are much older than your age, but in others ...' Marty, confused, disengaged the milking machine. The cow ambled out into the dark paddock.

'No, no, I don't mean *age!*' Alexa felt her voice grow harsh in impatience. If her mother couldn't tell her, who would? Dad had seemed to think Tod was no longer a boy, to let him go on the muster ... and Tod had said something about 'being a man ...' How did *they* know?

'I mean, is there a time, a thing that tells you when you're a woman. I think a lot of people think having babies means you are grown up, but I know you can have babies even when you're twelve, so that can't be right.' Alexa grew bolder, looked around the side of the cow. Her mother had fastened the cups on to the next cow, and was leaning against the wall looking out the door.

52

'Was that all you wanted to do, have babies, Mum?'

The challenge in her daughter's voice was unmistakable. Marty forced herself to think. Her child was asking something of her, and caused her mind to race frantically. What had she wanted? What did Alexa want? Through the darkness she pictured her daughter, her smooth face, her body so slender and tall. But her actions! She took in her breath sharply. When was the last time she'd heard Alexa giggle the high, happy sound of a girl? When was the last time she'd seen her playing? She couldn't remember.

'Yes, I have been happy raising a family,' she answered softly. 'That was enough for me. But you . . .'

'What about me?' Such terrible demand in that voice!

'Well, Alexa, you have more options.' Marty said the last bit in a rush. 'Things are different for you than they were for me. You have the opportunity to live whatever life you choose. To stay, to go away . . .'

'Oh, Mum! I wish, I wish . . . I wish I *knew!* I just feel like I'm sitting here, doing nothing, I just know there are things I want to do but I can't think what!' Alexa moved into the light, excited now. Her face in the dull glow had opened, the eyes bright like dark glass. Should she tell her, tell her about the otter? Maybe she could tell . . .

From inside the house, the baby wailed once and stopped. Marty lifted her head sharply, like an animal sensing the air. She listened with her whole body, not moving. The baby went back to sleep.

'Let's hurry, Lexa. I've got a lot to do before bed,' Marty said, tiring of the conversation. It exhausted and frightened her. Alexa felt the distance between them suddenly like a cold draught.

'Why did you do what everyone else did? You *must* have had other things you wanted to do!' Alexa surprised herself, attacking her mother. She wanted to lash out, force the answers from her. She shrank back into the shadows, her face flaming.

'I made my choice,' said Marty softly. 'No one has the right to question another person's choice. You must make yours. I can't answer your questions, and I can't be who you want me to be. But I am who *I* want to be. You have to accept that!' Marty softened the anger in her voice.

'I don't know what becoming a woman or a man means. I think it isn't really different; I mean, I don't think it is different for one or the other. I think it has to do with *seeing* things, how you *see* the world, and what you *do* with it.'

She walked over to her daughter, who looked so small crouched by the big jersey cow in the corner of the shed. She touched her shoulder, hesitantly. She wanted to hold her, as she had when she was a small child, rocking her and smoothing her hair and tears. But this was not a small child and there were no tears on that set, intense face. They stood poised for a split moment, and then Marty felt the hard body shiver, turn, push into her, and stand against her silently. She held her. She could only be her mother; she could be no more.

They carried the heavy milk containers into the house. Marty watched her daughter walk ahead of her across the yard. She had seen movement like that before, the still, careful movement before violent action. Once, at the tip of a spur, she had seen a young strong deer poised; she had seen the slow surrounding of the dogs about to attack and the careful tensing of muscles under the golden hide, and then the great creature leapt out, over the rocks. Marty had been afraid to look, to see if it had truly broken free, or if it lay mangled on the rocks below.

5

THE NEXT MORNING, Alexa woke in her room, knowing she would have to deceive her mother.

That, and the realisation that what she was planning to do was fool-hardy and dangerous, hit her like the tail-end of a disturbing dream slapping her awake. She sat upright in the cold room, staring out at the grey nothingness beyond the window-frame. Everything, even the huge macrocarpa windbreak, was obscured by the weight of fog. Something crackled under her pillow; she reached under and pulled out the map she had taken from her father's study.

In the blank quiet of the morning, no birds twittered from the dark branches, there were no squawks of chickens fluffing themselves in the warm dust of the yard. Everything was still. In that floating world, all the shadows shaped themselves to her fears and wishes. She sat, numb with cold, staring out until her eyes burned, waiting until the discomfort became too much, for then she would have to move.

'You have the opportunity to live whatever life you choose. To stay, to go away . . .' Her mother's words from the night before hung almost tangible in the dim cold of her room. Go. Go. Alexa got out of bed, dressed, made the bed and straightened the papers on her desk. She took her notebook, and the new drawing pad Billy had given her, several pencils and a rubber, and put them to one side. She draped the red scarf over them. She crumpled the false starts of her school term paper into tiny balls, and threw them into the basket by her desk. She moved surely, and thought to herself how calm she was. She thought: how simple it would be not to go! And she wondered at her start of fear at that thought.

Her first obstacle came before she'd left the room. Her mother knocked and came in. Alexa sat stiffly on the bed, feeling like a criminal.

'I'll be working on the fences in the lower paddock,' she said to Alexa. The baby was secured firmly on her back; she was dressed in old jerseys and from her belt hung pliers, clippers, heavy gloves. 'I really think you should try to get that paper started today, Lexa — it's due in a week. Keep out of trouble, and start tea around five. I'll be back around five-thirty.' She swung her rucksack over her free shoulder and left the room.

Alexa caught her breath. She needed the day to get a head-start: she'd be searched for, as soon as she was missed. She ran to the head of the stairs and called down to Marty.

'Mum! I thought I'd ride over to the Willis's — maybe I can borrow their typewriter, and they always ask me to tea!' There. She'd done it. It was a pure, out-and-out lie. But it would give her the time she needed, for the Willis station was a long ride, and she could not be expected to be back before dark. She held her breath, waiting for the word from Marty, saying, no she couldn't go, she was needed here . . .

'Well . . .' said Marty, pulling on her gumboots, but she was preoccupied, and she just turned and waved, and walked out across the yard. In another moment, she was only a ghost in the fog.

The release of tension worked like a sprung spring in Alexa. She raced to her room, flung the old rucksack on the bed. Her stomach was cold and tight, and it made her movements jerky. She pawed through her closet for her warmest jerseys, her rain gear, two old blankets. She wadded them up and stuffed them in the rucksack; they took up the whole space, and she pulled them out, forcing herself to be slow. Folded tightly, the blankets fitted with the other gear, with the drawing pad and notebook. She carefully put the red scarf at the bottom. Downstairs, in the kitchen, her mind went blank. She had no idea how long she'd be, or even where she'd be, other than a vague idea from the map. Her stomach was tight and she moved about the warm kitchen jerkily, unable to find anything. She opened the fridge, saw a partial leg of lamb, cold and grey on the platter from the night before. She wrapped it in a plastic bag, threw in some apples, a bag of bread. Would Marty notice that? She pulled it out and reconsidered. Hastily, she rearranged the area inside the fridge, so there was no gap. From a drawer, she took a long kitchen knife, a ball of twine and a crushed box of matches. She stuffed the map and her notebook into the pocket of her jersey and heaved the rucksack on to her shoulders. She was ready. She stood poised in the middle of the kitchen, torn between fear of having missed some essential in her packing, and fear that her mother might return. Still she could not think. Her mind felt like thick mud; impatient, she turned towards the door and went out into the foggy morning.

The old horse, Hobo, stood like a steaming megalith in the fog. He looked dwarfed in the empty home paddock where all the riding horses usually grazed, but as she neared him he moved towards her, and the movement revealed his massive size. He was an old horse, older than Alexa, older than Tod. They had taken their first ride on him, learned to ride on his broad gentle back. Jim could not bear to shoot him; he was his first horse, the horse he'd ridden when he'd first worked this station. Alexa leaned against him, suddenly worried. How strong *was* Hobo? He'd always seemed ageless and indomitable, but he must be nearing thirty. No riding on the station was easy, and off the edge of that map the lines of ridges and gullies seemed more defined, sharper, deeper. The horse shook his head and whickered at her. The noise helped her to decide; *he* was willing. She could trust him, as she had as a child. She heaved the saddle on him, tied the plastic bag on the back. Max, released from his kennel, waited eagerly at the gate ahead of them. She clambered on to Hobo's back and turned him towards the hills.

By the time they were well out into the endless tussock and

snowgrass country covering the sloping basin that was Jim's only decent grazing, the sun had burned the fog clear. The air was still cold, and the wind hissed through the grasses. Above Alexa, pipits hung suspended on the updrafts, trembling in the hard blue space as they filled the day with song. Alexa squinted to see them, but it was impossible to locate the tiny bodies in that blinding expanse of sky. Three or four hawks circled on separate levels of thermals, wings curved gracefully at the tips, great pinions constantly adjusting and re-adjusting to the air currents. They slid down one thermal, caught another, swooped up again.

'Dead sheep,' said Alexa making the connection. From habit she considered searching for it, for Jim had taught them to note any thing they saw on their rides and report it back to him. But Jim was away on the muster, and she wasn't going back — at least, not yet, not until she'd found her lake . . .

She urged Hobo into a bone-jarring trot, and then into his rocking, more comfortable canter. Might as well take advantage of the relatively easy terrain to make as much time as she could. The sense of urgency was strong. Once it was known she was gone they'd start to search for her. They'd think she was lost as people got lost all the time in the high country. Trampers, hunters, even sheepmen, were sometimes found frozen in gullies, or broken at cliff-bottoms. She felt her belly claw at her in fear. She leaned low over the great neck of the horse, trying to stop the cramping in her gut. She would not be afraid! She would not go home! The thought of turning home in fear angered and inspired her.

The hills had become steeper and Hobo had slowed to a walk on his own as he climbed through manuka scrub and the gnarled, thorn-infested bushes of matagouri. It was wild country they were heading for, lonely and silent except for the constant wind. Now and then, a small movement in the denser areas of bush would reveal a tiny flash of a fantail, or a curious black and white robin. Once, passing through a thicket of bush and tea tree, where the wind was unable to penetrate, she heard the fluted, water-pure notes of a bellbird.

The tussock thinned as the land rose even more sharply, and Hobo's hooves struck bare rocks. Ahead of them was a narrow saddle bridging the stone-grey ridges of two hills. The line of earth cut sharply against the hard blue of the sky. The going was treacherous now, the ground covered in loose shale and schist. But Hobo was slow and steady, and he dug in his great hooves carefully as he laboured up. There was a tiny tarn nestled in the hollow at the saddle's top, and as Hobo regained his wind, snuffling at the water, Alexa stared out across the narrow valley below. There, ribboned through the endless dun-brown hills, was the jewel-blue Waiau River. Even from the saddle she could see the white wind-caps on the brilliant surface. It was beautiful, inviting and terrifying. It was as far as she'd ever gone and was the cut-off point from the rest of the station; it was where one turned back. A great eagerness filled her throat. She would go on, into the jagged mountains beyond, through the eerie, moss-draped beech forests of the true high-country, and even further into the realm of the king of ranges, the blazing white Kaikouras. There, hidden in a pocket on those magic stark slopes, was a tiny, perfect lake, lying like the heavenly blue egg of a minute bird in an invisible nest. And in the lake, she knew . . . she knew . . ! lived the otter.

The wind was abrasive on the exposed saddle, screaming between the narrow cut from valley to valley, sweeping through the ice-cut slopes. Alexa put her hand on the strong warm neck of the old horse, felt the thrill of muscles and blood under the shaggy hide, felt him eager like herself, as if the wind brought him some promise. The immensity of the elements no longer frightened her as they had a moment back. She called to Max and he came to her. The animals were so alive and strong, and completely at home in the violent beauty of the land around her. They manoeuvred carefully down the slope from the saddle. Once they were in the small valley, they were no longer cut so sharply by the wind.

Beech forest grew in dark fingers up the steep hills,

beginning in dense thickets on the flat ground near the river. Alexa turned Hobo into the dim forest, through the creepers and moss which hung thickly from the branches and tree trunks. Once in the forest, however, she found whole areas open to the sunlight, the undergrowth stripped and trampled, the trees naked and thin. It seemed as if a machine had been there, slashing and ravaging great mouthfuls of the fragile place. But it was no machine. Almost at the instant Alexa knew the answer to the destruction, she saw it as well.

Standing taut, ready to leap, dappled at the edge of a clearing, was a small herd of red deer. Alexa caught her breath. They were magnificent! The sun speckled their bright hides as it fell through the upper leaves of the beeches. The muscles of the deer were bunched and rippled under their red-gold coats. So perfectly still were they, so beautiful against their deep-green surroundings, they might have been dreams. For a split second, neither the girl nor the deer moved. Hobo stood, ears pricked; Max stiffened in excitement. Then with a violent snort, the stag stamped his foot, shifting uneasily. His head vibrated as he lifted his top lip, drinking in the strong smell of the intruders. Alexa remembered uneasily that the stag would be in rut, temperamental and untrustworthy. Those thick-pronged antlers could disembowel a dog and even a horse with a single thrust of his neck, if he felt threatened enough to attack. The does gathered behind him as the stag took a step forward and stamped again. Alexa held her breath in awe and anxiety. The stag swung his head, as if catching her own uncertainty; he stamped once more and then turned and leapt through the gold and green wall of sun-splashed leaves into the dimmer centre of the forest, and was gone.

It was the red deer who had done the damage to the forest. They had stripped the trees of the protective mosses and lichen as far as they could reach on their hind legs, eating the tender second growth from the forest floor. They had eaten the leaves and vines and creepers, mashing down the soft loamy earth so that the worms could no longer aerate the soil.

The forest here was dying. Alexa knew the deer were trouble, not just for her father's sheep but for the conservation of the forests. The wild beauty of the deer tugged at her; the vision of their golden tenseness would not leave her.

How could it be that such beauty, such perfection, could be so destructive? Maybe it was true — just then she could almost sympathise with her father, there was no place for something as useless as beauty in this rough demanding land. Another vision imposed itself over what she had just seen: helicopters clattering their vicious roar low over the hills, hunters with long slender guns poised at the open door, and later, the same whine of the helicopter, higher up now, so the swinging net suspended below it, filled with the crumpled bodies of deer, could clear the trees. How distant it had been from her then, the death of those countless deer! But now, she saw in her mind's eye this small herd, the great dappled stag and the strong tall does, contorted and twisted in that hanging net sweeping above the hills. She shuddered.

'Come on, Max!' Alexa cried, turning Hobo to go. She wanted to be out of that forest, out into the great brightness, on to the river that was no longer the boundary of her day.

They stopped to rest on the river's bank. She wished she had a clearer idea of the time, for it seemed she had been riding forever, and that the day might never end. She tried to calculate, nervous. Had she come far? She tried to remember how far the river was from the homestead, how long it had taken her in the past. She studied her map, holding it on the pebbles so the wind could not tear it from her. With her hand she measured the space between the homestead and the line of the river, between the river and the tiny lake at the far corner of the map. She had more than half-way to go! She stood up, caught in anxiety, squinting at the sun. Was it really low in the sky, or was it just that the hills were so high around her?

Alexa tethered Hobo and walked along the river-bank. The water seemed shallow, breaking over mounds of pebbles. It had been a hot, dry summer, but she knew how deceptive the water could be. She and Tod had ridden out this far when they were younger, full of the thrill of adventure. She remembered them sitting on the bank, daring, bragging about how to cross it. Tod had bragged loudest. He would cross it, alone, he said; he'd come home and tell her about it. She remembered the heavy worry that perhaps he *would,* would do it without her. But now she was the one doing it alone, without Tod.

It was a wild river. The undercurrents were dangerous, the water wide and cold, fed with snow. The bank, too, was treacherous, the packed, hard-looking earth hiding pockets of shifting, sucking sand that could give way beneath one's feet. She swallowed, thinking of this, and stared around her. At a certain point the water seemed calmer, more gentle. She stepped carefully on to the sand, testing it. It dimpled but did not give way. She jumped on it; it was solid. She stuck a stick in the sand to mark the place and returned to Hobo. The horse stood happily in the warm sun, switching his tail, nibbling tussock. The high bank sheltered them from the wind, although the dull whine of it could be heard all around. Alexa leaned against a warm rock and ate an apple. She threw the core into the tussock and at once there was a screeching scramble from the dense patch of manuka near her.

Two keas clattered from the shadows and landed near the apple core. They screeched at each other, lifting their thick, blunt wings and exposing the bright orange patch under them. The ebony beaks clacked until one kea waddled off a short distance, to sit glowering at the other. The parrot tossed the core into the air, severing it with his beak and grasping the uneaten part in his claws. In a moment, the entire core was gone. Both keas cocked their heads now, surveying Alexa and the dog with bright, curious eyes. They stalked closer on their turned-in, oversized feet; one of them pulled at the leather straps on her rucksack which lay off to one side.

'You cheeky things!' she laughed at them softly. The parrots looked at her hopefully with their blackberry eyes. When she laughed more loudly, they answered her with their own shrill chortle. Another kea flew down and the three began to root busily in the tussock, throwing great bunches into the air as they did.

Alexa scrambled back on Hobo, called Max, and turned up the river to the crossing she'd marked. The big horse went willingly to the sand's edge, but balked at the suction under his hooves. The keas flew up screaming, as if trying to impart some message. Hobo snorted and shook his head, rattling the bridle bit.

'Move, Hobo!' spoke Alexa sharply. She dug her heels into the horse's sides and he lumbered out onto the sand, head down, blowing loudly from his nostrils. He swung his neck up and down. His hooves brought ominous sucking sounds from the black muck under the sand, and Alexa leaned over to look. The sand was holding, and once he made it into the water, the bottom would be reinforced with pebbles. Hobo snuffled at the water, hesitated, and then plunged down into the river.

It quickly became much deeper than the bright water had suggested to Alexa from the bank. Max was swimming strongly, and the horse pricked his ears, following the dog. The water frothed against his chest and filled Alexa's boots and soaked her legs. She hitched her rucksack high on her back and dug her feet deep into the stirrups. She clamped her knees about the horse and shouted at him, the shout to clear her head of her own fear as much as to urge him on. The horse lunged through the current, lurching on the uneven river bottom, and for one terrible moment, he seemed just to sink; and then he was actually swimming, and the freezing water folded about her, over her stomach and into her body. But in another moment, he found a foothold again, and they were rising slowly towards the far bank, and the wind was clawing its way through her wet clothing.

She had done it; she'd crossed the river; there was no longer any lingering thought of turning back. She'd crossed the river, the river that had always stopped her before. Tod had never gone this far. Oh, perhaps he'd be crossing it further down, on his muster, but it would be on a crude bridge she knew her father had built, at the narrow part. She sat straight on the dripping horse as he worked his way out of the shallow water. The massive hooves were scrabbling now at the slippery sand of the bank, and he slowly emerged from the river. The wind enveloped her in freezing folds. Hobo bunched his shoulders for the final lunge on to the bank, and Alexa felt a stab of pure relief.

The horse was breathing heavily. He took a step on to the bank, then another. Suddenly, Alexa was flung forward on to his neck, and the big animal plunged chest-deep into the soft muck. So fast did it happen that neither girl nor horse moved for a split instant, the horse sunk beyond his belly in the suffocating mud, the girl sprawled on his neck. In that instant, Alexa knew the horse was about to erupt in violent terror, the hooves which could crush a skull would thrash out, the heavy neck would be thrown up and out with a thrust to free himself.

In one motion, she rolled free of Hobo, landing on her side on the mud, rolling clear; grabbing for the reins which had been flung over his neck, she desperately threw them back out of his way. In his struggle, he could easily catch his legs in the leather, either breaking them or tangling them so badly he would die there in the mud. She lurched once more, keeping her body flat to give it as much surface as possible. Beside her, Hobo erupted into a frenzy.

Alexa dragged herself on to the solid earth beyond the mud. Soaked and mud-covered, she lay on her belly on the gravel panting. The cold bit her and she struggled up, turning then to watch the horse.

'Push, Hobo! Push!' she screamed at him, but her voice was harsh and whispering. Nevertheless, it seemed to calm him to hear her; his ears shot forward, then back. She kept talking to him as he lunged, throwing his feet clear, straining forward with his neck. The black muck sucked at him in awesome gulps; it seemed alive. But Hobo was three-quarters draft, standing over seventeen hands high, and was immensely strong. His hind hooves, searching for something solid in the muck that trapped them, found a submerged log, hooked, thrust forward. With a muscle-rending effort, a final lashing of the front hooves, he at last heaved himself free and stood, steaming and trembling, on solid ground.

Alexa was trembling now, too. She tore handfuls of dry tussock in clumps, rubbing the horse with it. Hobo stood calmly, breathing hard, content to let the girl scurry around him. She scraped and scrubbed at the horse, tearing up new tussock when the old handful got too wet. Hobo recovered faster than she, for he turned his head to her, lipping at the wisps of tussock. Her effort warmed her as well; she used some handfuls to scrape the mud from herself, and the wind, while cold, was driving the wetness from her sodden jeans. She realised her rucksack had been miraculously untouched during all this and she pulled out a blanket and wrapped it around herself. Her bag of food had disappeared from the saddle, either in the river or the mud. After half an hour of hard work, she felt warmer, drier, and reassured that Hobo was unharmed.

There was nothing to do but go on. She felt oddly deflated after the adventure. Even Max seemed quiet, trotting steadily behind the horse as they went on.

Later, when she looked back, she would know that it was then, after the river, that all remains of life on the homestead had disappeared for her. The first surge of satisfaction at crossing the river before Tod had left her, replaced by something deeper, ultimately more satisfying. She was now in completely unknown land, on her own. The animals, too, had become part of her — Hobo was no longer the horse she had to ride because there were no others: he was a great, breathing, alive animal who was with her and part of her journey. She could imagine no other horse. And Max, no longer something she needed to protect, to hide, but a strong intelligent animal. The focus of *proving something* had altered there on the river bank. This journey was no longer undertaken in anger, in frustration, in the need to prove she was as good as Tod. It was simpler now: it was to find what she knew was there. The otter. It was to find the thing which existed secretly and perfectly in its home, used by no one,

65

hunted by no one, known by no one except herself and Billy.

And the journey became, as well, its own reason, the excitement of the adventure luring her and compelling her. So they went on. She knew it was late afternoon now. The harsh, sunlit wind had dried her clothing except her boots, and the mud flaked from her and from the horse like grey skin. The gullies and scree-slides cut black passages of shadow into the rock. Manuka and matagouri sent long dark tendrils of shadow on to the golden, dusty earth. The tussock crackled under the hooves, stiffening in the cooler air. Alexa could see a massive wall of mountains ahead, dark, with the sun heavy and poised on the jagged rim. A steep saddle cut through a lower ridge, and another lay beyond, and beyond that she didn't know. She reached inside her jersey for the map and pulled it out. It was wet and black with mud, unreadable. She stared at it in dismay, trying to find on it some clue to get over what lay ahead. The golden sun lay heavy on everything, until all things seemed saturated with warmth and syrupy light. The world seemed to hang suspended.

There was nothing to do but search for a way over the great ridges in front of them. It quickly became steep. Hobo picked his way surely over the loose rocks and tangled scrub. Twisted shrubs grew far up the slopes here, and the roots clung to rock, tripping at the horse. The animal strained with effort, snorting, and Alexa slid from his back to lead him. Without the huge body to keep her warm, the wind cut into her. She felt tired for the first time, and when she became conscious of it, the thought exhausted her further. And for the first time, the thought of nightfall worried her. With the sun down, the air would become unbearably cold.

She almost panicked then, for it was suddenly obvious to her how badly prepared she was, how stupidly she had planned this journey.

'I'll find a place, I'll find a place, don't worry, don't worry,' she panted in a sort of chant as she grasped the mud-caked reins and struggled up, up. Numbly, she avoided the spiky grasses and sharp rocks. As the growth became sparser, the rocks and shale became more slippery, looser. Hobo's hooves rasped and scraped as he climbed behind her. Where was she going — *why* was she going? She stared up at the narrow saddle, as if it were a promise, as if some answer to the coming night lay just beyond it. She could not stay on the exposed slope where she was, so she could only move up.

At one point, she no longer had to look up to see the slope of rock cutting across the golden sky. They had almost reached the top. She stopped for a moment, almost afraid to reach it. Looking back, Alexa could see the hours of hill country she'd come through, a barren expanse of dun rocks, dun-brown tussock, golden sky and black rock. It was hard to imagine human beings other than herself here. She was alone; it could have been the moon. She swayed, dizzy. The dizziness turned to exhilaration; she could feel the pulse of her heart through her body. Alone! Just she was here, and the wild things: the deer and keas, the hawks and pipits, the rabbits, fantails, wild goats — all alone in this endless landscape of sun-soaked, dry brown earth. At the extreme edges of the horizon which formed a huge rim in all directions lay the mountains, golden-white or black streaked with white, stark and relentless and forever. The ridges were becoming obscured now with gathering mists.

Ahead, the saddle peaked and broke sharply. Just as they reached it, Hobo stumbled on a loose stone, falling to his knees and righting himself almost at once. Alexa caught her breath, but the horse jangled his bridle and walked on. When they reached the top, they stopped again.

The mountain they had climbed jutted down ahead of them in a long, steep curve. To her left, another mountain tumbled down in slashed cuts of grey and black rock. All around her, the mountains seemed to fall breathlessly down, down, falling to a tiny point at the bottom that was not grey or black but blue. It was so tiny and perfect, an oval-shaped point of blue ... so blue was the colour it seemed like a strange gem, so blue the eyes watered, so deep and bottomless a blue the breath caught on the edge of the throat the way the mountains caught on the edge of that brilliant point ...

67

And she knew it was water. It stirred at one end, grew into motion further on, frothed to whiteness, until it fell and tumbled through glass-green rocks into a shallow basin, filled it, fell again with a misty froth, and finally fell to a narrow gorge which curved away out of sight. And from some of the mountain sides, she could see icy streams crashing into the blue stillness. At other points, beech and ferns shadowed the blue and grew high up the slope above it. At some places, bare rock jabbed into the water, and at other places, a narrow beach curved into the blueness. Tiny clouds of mist whispered about the surface of the water, for the sun had left its surface long before.

She wanted to cry out, but could only stand, her hand tight on the reins, the dog pressed against her legs. It was water. It was a lake. It was *her* lake! And as she thought this, and stood staring down, the vision of an old man on a horse was with her, and her heart filled with emotion as she realised that Billy might also have stood here and that down there she might finally share his secret and prove his story. But now she was alone, exhilarated, looking at her lake, and it had been there forever, perhaps never seen before by any but the old man.

And when the reddening sun reached the rim of the mountain opposite her, rolled along the jagged edge, punctured, flattened and sank, she felt the cold stealing into her, felt the night coming behind her, and below her was the place she would be that night. So she started down. It took an ageless time, and when she got to the bottom, among the rock-slides and trees and mist, the water glinted at her, coldly welcoming, and the stars flinched against the black surface.

6

TOD HAD NOT imagined how dark and windy the nights in the hut could be. The men around him moved fitfully, snoring and grunting in their sleep. Tod, still awake, felt all alone. He felt the wind as much as heard it; it rattled at the tin loose on the corners of the roof, brushing the old tussock against the walls. Outside, the dogs were restless, sliding their chains through the dust, growling and whimpering. Once in a while, a man would half-wake, yell incoherently through the wall at the dog to shut it up.

His body was sore and he could not get to sleep. The images of the last two days stood out in his mind like persistent beacons, and closing his lids only made them more insistent.

His mind went over and over each action during those days. He didn't know how much of a help he'd been. It had been a longer ride than he had ever expected, with heart-thumping climbs through loose schist, scrambles down gullies lined with thorns and sharp rock, and then the interminable waits at the bottom of the beats where he stood holding the horses, listening for the faint cry from the man above him signalling that a mob of sheep was heading his way. After the cry, a tense wait, a command to the dogs, the sheep would burst through the scrub, wild-eyed, clattering through the slithering rocks, bounding down on piston legs. He would leap at them, waving his arms, heading them back down the gully towards the main group being held somewhere ahead of him. The sheep, some rolling in wool from having missed the previous year's shearing, were wild, breaking in all directions. The dogs would not wait for his commands, darting after the runaways, barking or snaking through the scrub. They were his father's dogs, and had been trained well; luckily they knew what to do. He rolled restlessly in the bunk. He knew there had been times when he hadn't been in control, had run madly, yelling at the dogs. He wondered how many of the other men had seen him make a fool of himself.

This morning, he roused himself, hearing a jarring clatter of someone beating a tin plate. Outside, the world was dark and closed, the last of the night filled with fog that covered the dogs with silver beads of moisture. The dogs pulled on their chains, barking and bickering with each other.

Jim grinned at his son.

'Ready to move out?' he asked, letting his arm drape casually over the boy's shoulder. It was the touch that said everything. He hadn't done so badly, then. Perhaps he'd even been useful!

'Lot to do before we leave,' continued Jim. He outlined the day's plans while the men shoved themselves into layers of clothing, leaving the most important item — their boots — until last. He copied every move, remembering Jim's words about boots, how they could make or break a man on a muster in the high country.

They rolled their gear into tight bundles, while from around the side of the shed came the smell of frying chops and potatoes. It was cold, so cold it settled in the men's bones as soon as the warm bunks were deserted. The men were in good humour; the last days hadn't been bad. The sheep had been gathered in twos and threes to form the small nucleus of what would be a huge mob at muster's end. They grazed silently in the fog, the crisp grass whispering under the sharp hooves.

It was good to sit around the fire with the men. The hut had no stove, so the fire was outside, the men sitting on their bedrolls or on the wet earth. Behind them, the eager dogs whined and grumbled. Sometimes a man would turn and speak to them, absently but with sharp, cursing affection. They all fiddled with equipment. Jim examined the radio, his most important and expensive gear. When the men split up, as they would that day for the first time, the radio kept them all in contact.

Billy drank his tea from a great enamel mug. Leaning low over to the man next to him, he said something Tod could not hear, and the man laughed.

Billy's stories relaxed the men, bound them together. Tod couldn't understand half of what he said, but when the men laughed, he laughed too. What a face that old man had, under his shapeless hat! It was so browned and lined it was like old leather, but smooth and somehow beautiful — not grizzled and unshaven as many of the old men Tod had seen on the station in his life. He thought it a good face, for it was so very old and yet, it did not conjure up those emotions connected with seeing age: pity, or embarrassment at a shaking hand, a toothless mouth. There was none of that. Tod studied him from the safety of the fire's smoke. Maybe he wasn't as old as he seemed. Dad said Billy was the best all-round sheepman there ever was. He said he knew more about any animal than anyone he knew.

He watched the men as they listened to Billy's story now. The voice droned, flat-toned, talking as he rolled his cigarettes for the day from the pouch tucked in his coat pocket. The men's hands were also busy, mending a boot, rolling a pack, their eyes always darting to the old man's face over the rim of a tea mug, or under their brows as they poked a needle through tough leather. They didn't all listen the same way. Tod studied them, wondering. The Pakeha, the white men, listened more lightly, laughed more easily, than the Maori shepherds. He watched the impassive faces of the Maori men, their eyes deep black, faces still. Why did that suddenly strike him? He wondered. And then he saw, in a flash of recognition, that those dark faces listened with the same intent, the same stillness, as Alexa listened. She, too, listened to Billy in that way, as if something depended on the story, as if she were gathering something secretly from those words. But they were just stories, an old man's stories; they didn't mean anything! The story ended, an impossible tale of a lizard who turned into a man. It was funny, and he laughed with the others, but this time he noticed once again the Maori men shifting, getting on with their tasks, but never a smile crossing their faces. He would ask Billy about it, later, if he had a chance . . .

Jim sent him with another young man to round up the horses. The paddock by the hut was a good ten acres, so they walked several minutes through tussock jewelled with mist. The boy beside him could not have been much older than himself, eighteen perhaps. Tod liked him, liked the jaunty way he walked.

'This your first muster?' ventured Tod.

'Naw,' the boy grinned, peeling a stick of gum. He offered it to Tod. They chewed in silence for a few strides, feeling strangely hushed by the dense fog around them. They could just make out ahead the quiet shapes of the horses, hear their soft breathing, the fluttering of curious nostrils. Now, a head bobbed up, then another; they could sense the boys' approach.

'You got a horse that'll come to you?' asked the older boy. He grinned again. 'Mine plays catch me. Takes twenty minutes to get a bridle on the bugger!'

'My sister's horse is around here somewhere. He's good mostly.' Tod whistled softly, using the same tone he'd heard Alexa use. The whole group was alert now, curious, ready for a good run-about in the fog.

Nelson's head swayed forward out of the dark mass of bodies. Slowly he ambled towards them, and nosed Tod's pocket. The boy gave him a barley sugar, smiling sheepishly at his companion.

'Promised my sister,' he explained. 'He's sort of her pet, you know? He's sound though; Dad says he's got the surest feet,' he went on swiftly, not wanting his new friend to think he'd ride a mere pet. 'But I promised I'd treat him special . . .' The older boy laughed, running his hand down Nelson's strong neck.

72

'Reckon nothin's wrong with that,' he said. 'Beats chasin' around for half an hour, eh!'

Tod slipped the bridle over Nelson's head and jumped on him bareback. He felt proud and strong, looking down at the other boy. They discussed their strategy for gathering the horses together in low tones, happily, both glad to have met. They could be mates, be on equal terms with each other, a relief from the slightly awesome company of the older men.

Tod circled behind the group, pushing the horses towards the gate. The older boy ran down the side, waving his hat, keeping them together. The hooves pounded hollow and muffled on the ground. It felt good to move, to stretch sore muscles and Tod moved the horses at a gallop. The horses felt good too; they bucked and squealed as they waited for the gate to be opened.

His friend's name was Hiwi Jackson, and he was younger than Tod thought — just seventeen. They stuck together like biddy-bids on a jumper: mates, grateful for each other's company. They saddled up together. With new-found confidence, Tod asked him about Billy's stories.

'Don't you think they're funny?' he said, curious.

'Why?'

'Well, you don't laugh, eh. Jack and Pete don't either.'

The other boy bent low to his horse's side, heaving on the cinch, straightening the stirrup. His dark face was blank, and his eyes were hidden by the hat he wore.

'Oh, I dunno,' he answered. 'Billy is . . . Billy don't tell 'em to be funny. Maybe they mean more to us, eh, than to a Pakeha. . .'

Tod tied on his bedroll, silent. He wanted Hiwi to be his mate; he wanted no distance, no secrets, between them. The other boy's face had lost the impassive blankness as quickly as it had come, and Tod felt relieved. He wouldn't bring up Maori subjects again; it caused a gap. It was a world he knew nothing about, although it surrounded him.

'Let's go!' cried Hiwi, hoisting himself up into the heavy stock saddle. The horse danced on the loose stones. Jim called over to Tod, and he turned Nelson towards him.

'We got to cover all the Red Block today, so I want you to stick with Billy. Dependin' what we get, and how fast, we may meet up tonight or early tomorrow.'

Tod stared at him in dismay. He thought he would be staying with his father. He stood silently as Billy walked up leading Bing.

'Keep your eyes on my mate, eh!' grinned Jim. Tod felt the blood storm into his face. They were treating him like a child! He threw a surreptitious glance back to Hiwi; the other boy hadn't noticed. He didn't dare protest and appear childish.

Billy stared him up and down with flat, dark eyes, as if measuring him. Tod stood defiantly. He could do as much as any of them, if they'd give him half a chance! Why had his father done this? Jim knew more about his own station than anyone; it was *he* Tod should stay with, learn from!

'Kinda mean, Jim, dumpin' the boy on me . . .' Billy's voice was as flat as his expression. Tod wasn't sure; he saw those eyes flash once, like a twinkle. He turned away in silence, choosing to be angry. He'd show him; he'd show Dad. They'd bring back more sheep that day than anyone!

'Tod, take Rose, she's got good bark, and you'll need her. An' take Fleet. Might be some close work up there in those slides.' Jim turned towards the other men.

Tod and Billy trotted out of the gully, Billy's silent blue collie a whisper behind the horses. Rose bounded ahead until Billy harshly told her to get behind. Tod compressed his lips; Rose was *his*, and his to command. They rode in silence, the horses picking their way through the scrub. As the ground rose, the fog faded to tendrils, then was gone altogether and the sun had already begun to burn.

One of the hardest blocks on the station to muster, it had been blocked in on the map with red pen by Tod's father, and the name 'Red Block' stayed. Four hundred acres of back-breaking spurs, gullies, rock-slides and shale banks, broken by matagouri so huge they could rip a horse's belly open if no care were taken. The wildest sheep lived there; some had eluded a muster for two years. If they survived the winters and the weight of wool on their backs, they became crafty,

74

fast, unpredictable. It might take two or more days to muster this area properly, depending on the weather, on how long the dogs and men could last . . .

The fog seemed to hiss off the hills with the intense heat of the sun. The great mountains in the distance loomed closer, blinding white, like something alive that marched forever around the rim of the world. In between them and the boy was an endless land of dun, gold and brown, and heat.

As the sun rose, so the rabbits appeared. The gully bottoms were alive with them. They saved their bullets for wild goats, for between the rabbits and other pests, the station was being eaten alive. Tod forgot his sullenness as he looked around him at his father's station, the land which would some day be his own.

'There's nothing here,' he whispered to himself. 'The rabbits have it all. God! Look at 'em!'

Billy turned in the saddle ahead of him.

'Not much for sheep, eh,' he commented shortly. Rabbits goats, deer — they all stripped the land of what the sheep needed. It was hard to believe anything could live here, but higher up the ridges they began to see signs of sheep, droppings, wool clumps in the thorns. But they were wild and fast, and they didn't see any of the animals themselves. Billy sent Rose in time after time, but she found no sheep to flush out. The sun got hotter, scalding their faces where the hat gave no protection. Billy shook his head.

'It's tryin' to fool us,' he said, looking around as they stopped to catch their breath. They were leading the horses now. 'Snow's around — I can smell it.'

They worked their way slowly to the top of a long, narrow spur. From there they could look out over the vast jumbled hills of the Red Block. Billy scanned for ten minutes with his binoculars, finally lowering them, grunting.

'Gotta go in blind,' he said. He sent Tod back down the slippery slope, leading the horses and taking the collies. He quartered the spur then, methodically, finding one, then a group of three. After two hours, they stopped to drink cold tea from their bottles. Tod sat dejected. Where were all the sheep?

75

He remembered the mob coming down from past musters, endless lines and masses of sheep. Maybe Billy wasn't so good, maybe he was too old . . . He never told him anything. How could he learn anything, if he wasn't told anything? All he was doing was following Billy, scrambling down slopes and climbing back up them. There seemed to be no method in it, no order.

They re-capped their bottles and started off again. The dogs trotted unevenly over the rocks and scrub. When the clumps of tussock and snowgrass became thicker, Billy sent Rose in more often. Finally, they began to gather a tiny mob together.

Straggling, in ones or twos, the sheep were collected. The going became even slower as the dogs worked to keep them together, to keep them from bolting back into the bush. After another hour they had fourteen sheep. How could all the sheep on the station be gathered this way? So much of it seemed governed by chance, thought Tod.

Billy worked silently, unless he was flushing out sheep. Then he yelled and waved his hat. Tod copied him with no sense of what he was doing. His throat was parched, and his boots rubbed on his ankles. The discomfort wore him down, but he was too tired to do anything but follow Billy and resent him. The old man was too old, couldn't cut it anymore. Well, he sure wasn't going to learn anything *this* muster, if he had to hang around Billy all the time!

By late day, they had a band of thirty sheep straggling out in front of them. The collies circled tirelessly, nervous, tensed, keeping the sheep together. They stopped so Billy could take his bearings and call Jim. He pulled up the aerial of the little two-way radio and flicked it on, calling out the code letters. The crackling from the radio sounded like flames through dry tussock. Tod leaned back and closed his eyes. Fleet and the blue collie held the mob quietly; the sheep were content now to nibble the thick snowgrass.

Jim was contacted. They would not be able to meet up that night. They were to take what they had and go on to the next hut and wait.

They worked their way slowly along ridges, down spurs. On one particularly steep ridge, the dark mass of ferns covered the gully below them and climbed the side of the next spur. They looked cool and alluring. The ridge was a treacherous one, filled with loose rock and shale, with caves formed by rock-slides pock-marking the slope. The dogs struggled to hold the mob together.

Tod led Nelson to the extreme of the group, close to the edge of a steep bank into a gully. A quick darting movement caught his eye. He stopped, peered below him and saw five sheep galloping through the rocks. A great ram with a huge curve of horns ran with them. How had it got in there? It was a truly wild sheep. Occasionally a lamb would escape detection, would grow up wild, never neutered or shorn.

What a magnificent ram it was! Its massive wool-cloaked neck was held stiffly back, arched, and the great thick horns curled out and around, extending almost to the eyes. It was a fine-blooded ram, he could tell, one of Jim's own, but wild and huge. He looked closer at the group now, they had stopped, wary, breathing hard. The others were all tagged ewes. He studied them through his binoculars and called to Billy.

'Have to leave 'em,' said Billy slowly, after looking into the gully. 'Can't risk a dog down there — too rough.'

Maybe for Billy's dog, but Fleet and Rose were good, sound dogs. He'd seen them ease sheep from difficult places before under Jim's whistles. And that ram! He knew Jim needed strong new stock. The station was poor, and rams, fine-blooded ones, were expensive to buy or raise. They had often talked of it, for Jim needed a tougher breed on this rugged land. He would bring this one back! How pleased his father would be! What did Billy know of this place, anyway? All day, he'd acted as if Tod didn't exist. As if he weren't really needed. Well, this was *his* time, his decision. He wanted the ram. He had a right to get it.

'Rose. Fleet.' He called them to him. The dogs waited expectantly.

He sent Fleet out to circle up above, so as to come on the sheep from the front. And he sent Rose straight down at them.

Rose was a seasoned, steady dog. She had always done what was asked of her. Her bark was deep and clean; she advanced calmly. She showed in her actions why Jim treasured her. At the boy's command, she turned eagerly for the gully, sighting the sheep immediately. But at the edge, she sensed something wrong. She looked down; it was almost a precipice in front of her. She hesitated, looked back at the boy.

Once again, his voice lashed out at her, higher now and more urgent. On reflex, she bunched herself to obey — but once again, the vicious drop in front of her stopped her. Above her on the hillside, Fleet raced back and forth, trying to find access himself. Gingerly, he ascended, hopping, scrabbling, casting about. He was young, very eager. He caught the flicker of movement below him: sheep! It excited him; he leapt for a rock, but it jostled, gave way, rolled and he was thrown.

Tod's voice cut into Rose. He was frantic now; Billy sat watching. Every nerve, frayed by the day of heat, frustration, and anger, jangled. His father's dogs could do it. He would bring in the ram. If Billy wasn't going to help, fine. Rose could do it. He hadn't heard Fleet yip with pain.

Rose tensed herself. She could see the sheep, bunched below her. She leapt for a rock, missed, twisted her heavy body for the next one. She hit it but could not gain a foothold. Down, down, from rock to rock to tussock clump, and she tucked herself instinctively against the blows, landing heavily against a thick clump of tussock. She tried to stand, then fell.

The ram swung his great head, rumbling. He was wild; no human being had touched him, no dog had held him. He lowered his head at the inert form in front of him. Out of the corner of his eye he saw another, smaller dog, darting closer, crouching, whipping back and forth. The ram bellowed and charged.

Tod stood paralysed above. What had he done? He turned, called Billy, but the old man was not there. The small mob of sheep became restless, hearing the noises below.

In panic, Tod began to ascend the cliff. The ram charged at the still form of Rose lying on the ground, but the little collie, Fleet, still held him back, a darting, tiny annoyance. The ram pounded the dry earth, swinging his head. Tod scraped himself on the sharp schist. Oh, let him hold him till I get there! he prayed inside himself. His breath whistled in his throat. No foothold. He was stuck. Helplessly, he crouched on a ledge. The ram bellowed again, charging.

Suddenly, that bulky body leapt in the air, twisting violently, and falling with a boom that shook the cliff side, he kicked once and lay still. Only then did Tod hear the echoes of a rifle. He craned around to look. Billy hung over the precipice, holding the gun.

Slowly, then, very slowly, Tod lowered himself down the cliff. Fleet held the remaining sheep fiercely with his yellow eyes. Tod was there now. Hoarsely, he whispered to the collie.

'That'll do, boy. Let 'em go. That'll do!' and he bent to stroke the slender black head. Rose still lay where she had fallen, but her eyes were open, clear, watching them. He cradled her broad golden head in his lap. She thumped her tail. Thank God . . . nothing wrong with her back, then. Maybe . . . maybe she was just winded. He felt over her carefully, feeling no broken bones. She never whimpered.

'Good girl!' he cried softly. 'Clever Rose. Good clever girl. You can get up, get up.' The dog lifted her head. Good. She thumped her tail again. She'd done what had been asked, done it well. The boy's voice told her that. He was calling her. More to do. She sighed, struggled up, shook her heavy fur. Where? Where to now? The brown eyes watched the boy.

Tod held her, crying. Above him, Billy still lay on his stomach, looking down at them. Eventually he stood up. He wanted to go down to the boy, touch him perhaps, tell him it was all right. But he couldn't. There was nothing he could do for him. The action itself would punish the boy for many nights to come . . . When he saw the tears, he turned away, went to get the horses. A man's tears were his own.

It took the good part of an hour to get under way, once the small mob was quieted, compacted, and the horses were gathered. The silence between them was heavy. Rose trotted wearily behind Nelson, no work asked of her. By the time they reached the little hut, it was dark.

Tod gathered wood for their fire in silence. As soon as the sun had gone, the cold was upon them, as if it had just lain in wait all day, biding its time. The wind beating down now from the mountains held more than the promise of snow. The flakes came, big and wet, softly.

They hobbled the horses, tied up the dogs close to the wall of the hut. Billy took Rose into the hut with him while Tod fastened blankets over Nelson and Bing.

The wind became increasingly violent as darkness descended, sweeping down from the mountains, full of icy snow. Tea was a miserable meal, with neither Tod nor Billy speaking. Billy appeared complacent, his silence seemingly ordinary. Tod felt like one of the dogs after a low reprimand. How could he have done what he'd done? How could he have endangered the dogs, his father's dogs, like that? He had been blind, blind with the sight of that ram — no, with his own stupidity, anger. Why had he been angry with the old man? He couldn't remember now.

As if reading his thoughts, Billy suddenly spoke.

'You all right now?' His voice was bland, without sarcasm or malice.

'It . . . it was too steep for her,' Tod whispered. The cold in the hut sharpened his guilt.

'Well, it all came right, eh. That's how you learn,' said Billy tamping down the tobacco in his rolling paper. 'Every man's gotta test his dogs, sometime. I've done . . .' The old man began to doze, pushing his legs out in front of him. The boy would never needlessly endanger his dogs again. It was a big lesson. He opened his eyes once, peering at the boy. He liked him. It would be a long cold night for him.

'I don't know why — I can't remember — I just saw that big ram, eh! Dad wants rams. I wanted to get it for him.' In a rush, to hold off the tremendous howl of the storm outside, he went on. 'I didn't mean to hurt Rose. She's one of Dad's best dogs!' He was tense with the agony of remorse, with the fear

80

of what might have happened. Billy felt the tight body of the boy in his own heart. Let him work it through. It's terrible pain, those tests you set yourself, and lose. Let him go through it; he'll sleep. The bite's always gone a bit, come morning.

'It came right,' he said again to the boy, in his soft voice, fondling Rose's ears. 'Rose did herself proud, eh, old girl?' The dog folded up happily by his leg. Untold luxury, to be allowed inside.

Outside, the storm careened in over them, shaking the hut windows, booming in through the dark beeches. The dogs curled together in their hollows, and the two horses stood with backs to the wind, stealing heat from each other's body. The sheep, penned in a small paddock sheltered by the trees, hunched patiently together. Winter had begun. Tod fell into an exhausted sleep.

7

FOR THE REST of her life, Alexa would associate the colour grey with cold. Cold and hunger. She woke suddenly, as if a noise had disturbed her, but as she lay for a minute, she could hear nothing around her. Even Max, curled around her back, lay breathing softly. It had to be early — it was still very dim through the cracks in the front of the cave. She dared not move, afraid that any motion would heighten her cold and hunger to an unbearable point. She looked around at her cave. Max had found it. It was very low; she could not stand up fully. It wasn't more than a crevice in the rocks; it was long and narrow and must have been old, for moss grew near the opening, and the rough walls were covered with lichen. Strangely, it was dry. She patted the coarse sand and pebbles which were the cave's bed. Slowly, she sat up, groaning with cold and stiffness. Max stood, shook himself. She leaned forward in her blankets and felt her boots — they were dry! She felt a surge of joy, as if this small victory caused a new supply of energy to course through her. She put them on, still stiff with dry mud, and crawled out of the cave after Max. It was grey-dark, but the dawn would soon flare over the black mountains towering around her; it would be a clear, crisp day. There was no fog.

She examined the rock-slide over her cave. Carefully, she climbed up on the rocks, scanning the tumbled stones, testing them with her boots. If it were an old slip, as old as it seemed to be, the stones would have all shifted and settled by now, and there would have been no danger of being crushed in the night as she slept. Deposits of earth had formed in small crevices and pockets; tiny alpine plants grew in the dirt, even a hardy beech sapling was struggling to gain a hold in a tiny hole of earth. The rock-slide had happened a long time ago.

'Clever Max!' she said to the dog who was sniffing the cracks beside her. 'How did you find this place? If you hadn't just sniffed it out, we would have frozen, I reckon!' The dog wagged his tail, never stopping his exploration. It was true. She remembered the night before as if it were a dream, in dream-like shades of greys and blues and shadows. The careful descent down the mountain, down, down, towards that point of unearthly, depthless blue, surrounded by pinnacles of black rock all around. She had moved even then as if dreaming, slowly and carefully, her mind blank with wonder and exhaustion, the great body of the horse shifting and sliding beside her. She had no thought of any move save getting to the bottom, and once there, she had stood helpless and tired. The dog had explored on his own, and when he had disappeared for what seemed like an eternity, she had numbly begun to look for him. He was sniffing in the rock-slide, a dark jumble of stone and black shadow. Max had gone into one of those shadows, and that had been the cave.

Now, feeling awake, with an alertness sharpened by hunger, she bounded down the rocks toward the nearest thicket of tea tree. So thick was the dark green growth she could not even see the horse, but when she called out he whickered immediately in reply. Sheltered from the wind and cold, the horse had spent the night tethered in the thicket, and now he was as hungry as she. His need was more easily answered, for snowgrass and tussock grew thickly near the edge of the gravel shore. She saw there was no need to tether him, for the rocks and mountains formed a natural boundary all around.

Sunrise brought sounds with it; the beech forest that covered much of the flat and climbed the mountain from which the rock-slide had tumbled, stirred and whispered with life now. From its mossy interior came occasionally the flute-like warble of some bird, the twittering of yellowheads scratching about the soft forest floor, the raucous cry of a kaka. Light came suddenly. Alexa stood transfixed. It was as if, in a single instant, the mountains suddenly let go their rule of darkness, surrendered to the day, and became translucent with ice, patches of brilliant snow high up on the sides, and the greys which had seemed so flat and dead now seemed full of light and life. The glossy needles of the tea tree, the stalks of yellow tussock, the turning leaves of beech, all in an instant of brilliance became alive and wonderful.

And the lake! For the first time, Alexa turned toward the shore. It was like an alive thing, like a creature to be spoken to, and she addressed it.

'I'm glad I waited!' she cried. 'I waited till the sun came up! How beautiful you are!' She ran down the beach until her boots touched the water's edge. She felt as if she might be worshipping something. The lake held secrets, had tales to tell, and she would wait, wait until it was ready, and then she might know, too. She bent and scooped a handful of water to her mouth; it was so cold it burned in her throat, but it was wonderful to her. Her stomach contracted violently with the cold, and she realised she hadn't eaten in more than a day. The first thing she would have to do was find food.

'There must still be berries . . . and I reckon if I went down to the stream there'd be *koura* . . . an' there's bound to be something in the bush. . . .' She hadn't quite brought herself to realise *what* she would find to eat in the bush, for what was edible was what the birds ate, and what the wild pigs rooted for: grubs. The idea of *koura,* or freshwater crayfish, was not at all unappealing, so she called Max and started down the lakeshore towards the far end, where it tapered into a wild, rocky stream.

The sandy beach near the cave was quite short, and very quickly she found herself clambering over rocks and threading her way through dense undergrowth ringing the beech forests. She thought the place was like a hidden world, a sort of alpine Shangri-La, for it struck her that this lake was laden with life, and that the beeches and ferns and low shore-rocks stirred constantly with noises, calls and rustlings. She found herself wondering at this suddenly, because she remembered past tramping expeditions with Tod to some of the smaller ponds on the station near the homestead, and nothing had been as rich with growth and living things as this.

At one point, the shore became swampy, and there were rushes and *raupo* choking the black water. She took a stick and poked into the mud, seeing what could be stirred up, and there was a flurry of movement, a squawk, and the flash of white as a pukeko streaked away on long red legs. She laughed. The bird must have been crouching still at her approach, for she hadn't seen it.

'Pukeko,' she mused. They were silly birds, and couldn't fly well — maybe she could catch one, set a trap. She studied the swamp. It was very wet, with large areas of weed-choked water, and she had only her one pair of boots. She couldn't risk getting them wet again. She took off her boots and socks, and tested the water with her foot; it was so cold it numbed her immediately. Frustrated, she sat and stared glumly at the swamp.

Hunger started her out again. The lake was larger than it had seemed the night before. Crossing the swamp proved easier than she thought. It drained into a small stream closer to the lake's edge, and she was able to jump across.

At many points, the forest dipped right to the edge. With the sun out, it was a lovely, dappled place on the outskirts, gold and green, glossy-leaved, draped in spidery mosses and wrapped in creepers. She remembered it from the night before, and shivered slightly; it was an eerie, black place then. Several times, as she passed through the over-hanging trees, she heard rustlings that were more than bird noises, and she looked about anxiously. It could only be wild pigs or goats; they were the only animals large enough to crash through undergrowth like that.

Finally she heard the roar of water falling through rocks, and saw the mist-froth where the lake narrowed and fell through rocky pools. Bright green weed swayed in the water, anchored firmly to mossy stones. It was colder here, too, damp and slippery. Alexa climbed using her hands, bent almost double, for fear of falling into the rushing stream. She searched for a wider place, where the water would be less wild, for she thought it would be more likely the *koura* would be hidden in the calmer water under rocks. Max bounded with her from rock to rock, scrambling with his paws for a hold.

'Max, get back!' she commanded. It made her nervous and she was afraid the crayfish would scuttle further out of reach if they sensed danger. The dog scrambled back to a firmer rock and lay watching her.

The sun was blinding against the water and she had to squint, relying more on her hands to feel under the stones for the crayfish. After ten minutes of nothing but hands with no feeling, she sat to think, sticking her hands in her armpits and rocking back and forth with the pain as the blood came back.

'The funny part is,' she said to Max, 'I am cold and hungry and I'm not sure how to get out of here — but I don't really *want* to. I like it here!' The dog stood up with her, as she stood, feeling an absurd impulse to spread her arms wide and take in the whole place. It was true. This was *her* place; she had found it, alone, and there was the tantalising promise of the place which filled her richly.

When feeling returned to her hands, she tried again, more methodically. She lay on her belly on a rock and hooked her toes over the edge, peering into the eddying water and poking with a stick. There! A quick dart, a flash of brown and a tiny mist of disturbed sand. *Koura*! She struck the sand, grasped, and felt the hard carapace, the pinch of small claws on her finger. In triumph she pulled the crayfish up. It was tiny, hardly three inches — one bite. She put it in her pocket alive, where it squirmed against her belly. She took the jersey off and put it beside her, and began to search again. This time she had better luck, and found three. She stopped, considering how many bites she would need to fill her. With an hour's search, up and down the stream, she had found twenty *koura,* and her jersey pocket could fit no more.

In the cave, she built a crude fire, and roasted all the *koura* in their shells by sticking them in the flame. They took a long time to eat, for the carapace had to be peeled back and each minute piece of flesh picked out, but after ten, her hunger had dulled and she was able to eat more slowly. Twenty bites of food was good, but she knew it would not last long. It gave her time to search for firewood, and for something to warm up her cave.

She checked on Hobo, grazing at the far end of the little beach. When she called him, he came towards her, and she saw with a flash of fear that he limped badly, at times not touching his front hoof to the ground. A pebble, perhaps, lodged in his hoof? She wished it to be that, and not a more serious strain. She suddenly remembered his stumble at the saddle-top, and the difficult descent down the slope afterwards. But her worst fears were realised when she reached him, and felt the hotness of his skin around the knee, and saw it was badly swollen.

'Oh, Hobo,' she whispered. She was sick with guilt at having brought the old horse so far, when he had come so willingly. She ran to the lake edge but found only clean sand, and had to run down to the swamp for the thick black mud she knew would help the swelling. She ripped a narrow strip from the edge of her precious blanket, plastered the mud on his leg and held it in place with the cloth. She didn't know what else to do, or how serious the lameness was. She did know, for certain now, that she would not be able to ride out of this place.

'I reckon they'll just *have* to find me now,' she whispered again, holding the big head of the horse in her arms. Somehow, the thought of that did not bother her as it had the day before. She wondered at it: here, her life was in danger, there was little food, she might never be found, but she had lost the terrible, empty feeling of restlessness she seemed to live with daily at home. She did not feel aimless here.

She sat in the warmth of late morning, resting. The

drawing pad Billy had given her lay on her knees.

'I don't know what I'm here for, but I know it's something important,' she said aloud. The sound of her voice comforted her, and helped her straighten her thoughts. She wondered if she'd meant *here,* by the lake, or just *here,* in general, in the world. She decided it was the same. She turned to the first page of the pad. It was clean and new and flat; she smoothed her hand over it in a caress. She wondered if she could remember people's faces — they all seemed so far away. Was it really just yesterday she had left the homestead? She shut her eyes tight, trying to conjure up faces, Marty's, Billy's, Tod's — even Clive's. Her eyes flew open. She remembered Clive's face clearly — tanned and thin, lined with sun and wind, older than his twenty years, light-grey eyes, smile, and a broken tooth. She sat still and allowed herself to remember, and her stomach did not knot up this time. She just felt warm, as if she could feel the blood moving through each vein. After that, the others came more easily: her mother, with big bones, dark eyes, and Tod's face, like a boy's. And then Billy. His was the best, all lines and creases, and warm browns, wide thick mouth, soft ... black, black eyes and heavy brows. She saw she was drawing the face, surely, with broad strokes of the soft pencil.

'I think it's all right to like Clive,' she said to herself as she drew. It made her feel brave to say it, and strong. 'I just am not marrying anyone, that's all.' Billy's face stared back at her as she spoke, for her pencil had formed it well. She stared back at it.

'I don't want to be a farmer, Billy,' she told the drawing. 'I don't want to marry a farmer. But I don't want to leave — this ...' She stopped, confused. She did not want to leave the mountains, the rides on Nelson, the magic of sunrise over the Kaikouras ... but it wasn't for her. It was not really her place. Her pencil idled over the paper. Once more, the sinuous, long forms appeared as they had before when she allowed the pencil a will of its own. This time she concentrated, added a broad head, deep eyes: it was an otter. She had never seen an otter. She stood up.

'Otter! *Kaurehe!* I know you live here! I know you are here! Otter!' she called. Her legs were stiff, and she realised she could not sit idle for too long. Her survival depended on warmth and food. She decided on warmth for now.

Inside her little cave, Alexa smoothed the sandy floor and took away the largest pebbles and stones, putting them in a small pile. She gathered a few more small round rocks from the shore and brought them back. When she had scooped a good hollow near the entrance inside the cave, she lined it with flat stones, and then built up a rim with the round stones. She left a small pile of round stones near this, for she knew that rocks held heat for a long time once they had been in a fire for a few hours. Then she called the dog and headed into the beech forest. She was beginning to feel hungry again, but she was more worried about the promise of a cold night ahead.

The beech forest was dark and still inside, the birds silent at midday, the heavy rustlings from the forest further down the lake not present here. Alexa pushed her way deep into the interior, working her way up the slope. The trees hung thickly with great swaths of greenish moss, sometimes draping down almost to the forest floor. Vines and creepers and thick masses of fern made her progress slow. The floor of the forest was springy and dense with matted, decaying vegetation, rotting stumps, fallen clumps of moss. There was a heavy damp sharp smell of active decay. It was as if the world had forgotten this place, gone on without it, so ancient and primeval did it feel to her. She stood still, and found she was holding her breath. It was both oppressive and magical. As she stood, the forest began to stir around her; bright, quick flocks of yellowheads flitted among the vines and tree trunks, scratching for insects. Above her, hidden in the high branches, a kaka screeched. A curious fantail flipped up and down quite close, and she relaxed at the familiar squeak. She began to gather the moss, finding the driest clumps she could. Piled against the walls of her cave and matted around her at night, it would provide good warmth.

It was heavier than she thought to carry an armful back

through the tangled forest to her cave, and she saw she would need to make several trips. It was tiring and awkward work. She began to think of other foods she could eat. The roots of the fern could be pulled and eaten raw or roasted. She kicked over a rotting log with her foot and watched the scurry of myriads of beetles and grubs at the sudden intrusion of light. She swallowed. How hungry would she get here, before she began to eat those? Billy ate grubs, she knew. He used to tell her and Tod, and would laugh at the faces they made. Roasted, he'd say: crunchy and nice. She looked again at the whitish grubs, saw how fat and meaty they looked. Her stomach turned over in both hunger and revulsion. Well, she knew where they were — she'd wait till she was really starving!

It made her think of home, and of her mother. She felt a moment of sick guilt. By now, Marty would be beside herself with worry. Alexa imagined her in the kitchen, holding the baby against her, sitting still and quiet the way she did in real fear, like the time Jim had been gored by a bull and she was waiting for the helicopter to take him to hospital. She didn't cry or pace or have hysterics. She simply sat, straight, still, waiting, impassive. Would she be sitting like that now, or keeping food warm in the oven for the hungry men who would work in shifts looking for her?

Alexa brushed her hand over her face angrily. She couldn't think like that now! She was here. She'd had to come; she knew that. And now there were more important things to do than wallow in guilt. She gathered up a large pile of moss, stumbling as she stood up. It worried her to notice how dim and grey the beech forest had become; it was already late afternoon. She sniffed the air; it was sharp and cold. It smelled like snow.

She had come much farther this trip. She started back, a nameless dread welling up in her for no reason. She tried to shake it off, telling herself that it was because it was getting dark in the bush. She could not rid herself of the fear, and suddenly knew it was because she had not seen Max for some minutes, so caught up had she been in her thoughts. She tried to call him, but the fear stuck the sound in her throat. She felt something here. Where was he? She dropped the moss.

Alexa crept forward like a small animal, ready to freeze at any moment. There was a small clearing, dim and soft, with the stillness of movement about to erupt. Then she saw Max bristling, light glinting on raised fur, his teeth exposed, crouching half-hidden in the ferns. And beyond him and black-gleaming, sharp feet dug deep into earth, stood the boar.

He was beautiful and terrible. He was as black as the forest and his thick coat shimmered in the dusk light, his massive curving tusks jutting out over the strong snout. He was pure strength, perfect bulk. His tiny hooves jabbed the earth, braced. Leaves and moss clung to his huge head, hung from the muscular nose. His eyes were small, intelligent, angry. Slowly, he moved, slowly he lowered his massive head and swung it, the mouth parting, foaming, showing even razored teeth.

Alexa opened her own mouth; it was dry and hard to move. She tried to call Max off. She didn't know if she could. No sound came. It came to her then that this fight would be so awesome, so *magnificent,* and in her pulse she could already feel the quickening, as if she and Max and the boar were one — and she could not, would not, call him off. This was his test, her dog, her sook-dog whom everyone knew was a coward . . .

And when the dog and boar finally met, she could feel her own body tense as if she, too, had moved into the violence. She grasped a vine and swayed, feeling weak. The dusk had taken over now; there was only darkness and deeper-than-darkness which were the bodies of the boar and dog. They had closed silently with each other, teeth to tusk, hooves to claw, almost evenly matched in size. The ground rang with their weight and struggle. The mass fell apart, became boar and dog, stood poised on one breath together, and in one breath closed together again.

Alexa heard a yelp, a squeal, and saw the thrust of tusk into thick fur. She saw the slash of teeth into massive jowl, heard the grunt of surprise, but there was nothing she could do. The dark made forms larger, the ancient forest made them appear primitive, like dinosaurs. The mass again separated, and one huge form crashed off while the other lay still in a matt of ferns. Her fear returned with a gasp in her throat and a clamp on her heart. Alexa forced herself forward, to the still-lying form. She knelt, as if in slow-motion, and cradled the soft head in her arms, stroked the thick fur. The eyes were open, looking at her. She felt Max all over, more frenzied: where was the warm stickiness she knew she'd find? She shoved her hand under him, tried to lift, but he weighed over six stone and she could not budge him. He whimpered.

'Max!' she cried, then, 'Max! Get up! C'mon, get *up!*' She stroked him; there was no blood. She was sure of it. How could that be? She'd seen the tusk, almost felt the goring of flesh. She was sure: there was no blood. She felt his rib-cage, his legs, saw his head move. She stumbled to her feet, calling him.

The big dog sighed, thumped his tail, stood. He shook the ferns and leaves from his coat, limped a moment, wagged his tail again. When she gathered her last pile of moss, and walked back down towards the beach and the cave, it was as if nothing had happened. She felt each step in the forest stabbing fear through her. She hurried. Stories, her father's, flooded her: pig-hunts, the pigs treacherous, clever, blood-mad, moving their great bulk through the bush silently, doubling back, waiting ... And the dogs, ripped open by the sudden attack, screaming. But Max was unconcerned, and took the lead, and she could only follow him until at last she reached the edge and the beach.

There, it was not as dark as she'd thought, although the sun had sunk below the rim of mountains. She crammed the moss into the cave and felt her hunger well up in her. She would never find crayfish now in the evening, so she pulled up ferns, washing the roots in the lake. It was not a tasty meal, but it stopped the hunger pangs. She built a fire in her fire-hole and laid first sticks, then rocks, then more sticks, and finally moss. It would burn hot and low, she hoped, heating the rocks through. She jammed a blanket and moss in the crevice entrance, leaving only a hole at the top for the smoke to escape, and left, thinking how quickly her small home would heat up for the night.

Alexa went to check Hobo, and to tether him back in the thick scrub for the night. His limp was still pronounced, and the mud had hardened, but the swelling was down and the leg was not hot. She led him into the bushes and tied him, then took the other blanket, wrapped it around her, and went to sit on a rock by the lakeside.

The day had been a lifetime. Alexa found she could think back to herself two days ago, and yet it was not herself; the problems and emotions of that girl, while they were remembered, were not hers, and she could no longer feel them. Going on the muster . . . had she *wanted* to? But why? Here she was, in this place which was somehow hers, and she could no longer imagine being with the men, grubbing about on the hills after sheep. She thought of Max. It was not, she realised suddenly, that he had suddenly found courage to fight the boar: the courage had always been there. Only her father had labelled him a waste, since he did not follow the direction he was told to go, and be a sheep dog.

She leaned her chin into her hand and gazed out across the steely surface of the lake. The sky had turned black-blue, and the first of the evening stars had come out and were reflected on the water. The surface was still as glass. Alexa stared, mesmerised by the star on the silent surface, and when it rippled, when it shattered into a hundred tiny lights, she at first thought it was her eyes tired from the day and unfocused.

But she heard it, too, an almost-inaudible trilling of water on water, a whisper of ripples streaking on the black surface, breaking the star-light. She sat up slowly, forgetting to breathe.

The head broke the surface, a broad, flat, sleek face, thick whiskers each touched with the light of a rising moon. The eyes, deep and black, gleaming and alert. Then the body, like a thick snake, long and round and sensuous, curving on the surface with beads of water like transparent jewels falling from the slick fur.

Prince of the night-lake, the otter came, watching her from those space-black eyes, watching from the starlight mirrored in his eyes; lean and slender in the water, he watched her. Silently, the lake held him, its deepest secret, its deepest life.

'One day, I saw him.' Only, it was night. And it was she who saw him. She wanted to slide herself into the water silently beside him, swim to the blackness of night, feel her body slipping through folds of darkness and water, warm and sleek and perfect. The moon was up. The moon was in the lake, rippling with the otter. The water sang with the faintest whisper, the black eyes blinked; she buried her face suddenly into her arms.

When she raised it up, hot with tears, eyes bright from being too full of all she had seen, the otter was gone. She felt a rush of relief; the beauty, the promise, had been too great. Next time, she would be ready. Something stirred at her foot, flipped on the sand. She looked down, blinked. An eel lay gleaming darkly on the pebbles. Its gills fluttered, the slippery purple sides pulsed. It was as long as her arm, almost dead, and when she picked it up, cold and slimy-rubbery in her hand, she saw the tiny, perfect tooth-marks on either side of its head.

She took the otter's gift and went to the cave to eat, with the wind in her face and the first burn of snow light on her skin.

8

THERE HAD BEEN no dawn that day, although Tod had woken at four and been out on the hills since five-thirty. The snow fell as it had all night, fine and fast. Billy seemed to sense the ground beneath them, making his way slowly up the spurs, through the drifts. Tod could only follow, breath searing in his throat from the cold. It seemed to him they had been searching like this for an eternity, and that the day had not advanced. For hours, in the same grey swirling cold, the dogs had moved ahead of them, sniffing and scrabbling in the ice and snow. Rose, recovered from her fall the day before, could be heard barking cleanly through the gloom long before they would ever see her. Searching for sheep stranded in the drifts was heart-breaking work, and when, after hours, they had a tiny band of eight, Billy signalled back to Tod to turn around. It would be unsafe to go too far from the little hut in this storm.

'Better to wait. When it lets up, we'll go raking,' said Billy. The ice crusted his hair and the wool of his coat. And when they had slowly, finally, reached the hut, the snow was still falling.

Billy stripped off his boots and hung them above the cold stove. Tod stirred the dead embers, threw in the chunks of tea tree laid inside that morning, and lit it.

'Reckon I'll call your dad,' Billy said. He fiddled with the radio, the static sounding like the dry wood burning in the stove. He called the code several times and Tod leaned close as Jim's voice came through.

'Can you bring your mob over?' said Billy, 'There's a windbreak here — snow's not as deep, I reckon, as up there. Can't tell how long she'll last . . .'

The radio crackled violently. Tod could hear a voice, but only catch snatches of words.

'What's that?' called Billy, pointing the aerial about.

'. . . can't leave . . . Marty . . . call . . . lost. Copter's about here . . .'

'What? Dad! What?' Tod reached for the radio. Something was wrong! What had his dad said? Mum! Maybe something was wrong with Mum! He desperately shook the radio.

'Marty called . . . Alexa's been gone all night . . . took Hobo. Helicopter's picking me up when the snow clears . . .'

Billy answered now.

'Repeat slowly, Jim . . . we couldn't get it all.' Tod held his breath to catch the words. Alexa gone? Where? How far could she get on that old nag? The static cleared briefly, and Jim's voice filled the little hut.

'. . . said she was goin' to the Willis's, but she never got there. Couldn't even get the rescue party out till now, snow's so bad. They're tryin' to get a helicopter in to get me. Where the hell is that kid . . .' The radio had another spasm of static, Billy waited patiently and eventually, between interference, they planned the next moves. The remaining men would bring the mobs down to the gully hut on the Red Block where Tod and Billy were. There they would all wait until the snow cleared. There was enough grass in the gully and shelter from the wind for the whole mob. Then they would begin snow-raking, the slow clearing of paths for the sheep to come down. Jim and one other man were going back to join the search party and Billy was now in charge of the muster.

Tod spoke briefly to Jim.

'Don't you need me to help look, Dad?' he asked.

'I need you with the men now, mate. Reckon you'll be the best help to me right where you are . . . you an' Billy the best men I got! And don't worry . . .' The voice was cut by static. Tod clutched the radio frantically.

'What? What?' he cried.

'. . . said, don't worry. She's a smart kid, lots of sense . . . she'll be all right . . .'

They switched off the radio and the hut filled with an overpowering silence.

Billy pulled his boots off their hook and put them on.

'More wood now, eh, now we'll have guests . . .' he said. Tod stared at him. Wasn't he even worried? Alexa! All alone . . . in this snow! He felt sick with worry and fear. Billy ran the whetstone over the axe blade. After a moment, he stopped, looking at Tod from under his shapeless hat. He saw the young face flushed with worry, hands fiddling with helplessness.

'Otter,' said Billy, softly. Tod's mouth dropped open.

'She went to find the otter,' said Billy, as if to explain.

The old man was crazy! He was up in this hut with a crazy man! He sat heavily on his bunk, watching Billy methodically sharpen the axe. He stared down at the crumpled blankets on the bunk, thinking of the last time he'd spoken to his sister. His hand smoothed the blankets; they lay in ridges and lines of cloth, like the mountains on a map . . . Map! He'd shown her the map! She'd been fascinated, her finger tracing the lines, up, up, to the edge of the paper, to the tiny oval lake in the corner . . . He remembered in a flood of images now. He remembered the conversation in the kitchen, and he'd laughed at her . . . something about *otters*! He jumped down and stood poised on the floor. Billy looked up. Such an old face, old and brown, brown fingers deft and still now on the axe.

'There's a lake . . .' began Tod. Billy watched him.

'That lake — she kept looking at this little lake. You know, on the map. I showed her where we were going . . .'

The old man swirled the stone lightly over the gleaming blade.

'She went to find the otter,' he said. 'I told her about seeing one, once. It is something that is hard to see; she wanted to find it.' His voice was so calm that Tod was shaken.

'You *told* her? *You* saw one? Where?'

'I saw one,' answered Billy, getting up.

'But *where*? Don't you see? She's lost! You got to tell me where!'

Billy stopped at the door.

'I don't remember,' he said.

When the old man had gone, Tod spread the map out on the floor. He found the little lake quickly; it almost leapt out at him, now he recognised it. It was way to the west, a full day's ride from the homestead, and in the opposite direction from the Willis station. And on old Hobo . . . could he get that far? He switched on the radio — static. He called out the code to his father's group. Nothing. They would be on their way here, then, and Jim would have left. He tried the code for the homestead and again got only static. Of course . . . his mother would be tuned in to the search band, or else be by the telephone.

He sat helplessly, the radio growling intermittently in his hands. He switched it off. He *had* to let someone know; he knew where Alexa had headed. He studied the map again, figuring out the most likely route. Did she have a map? If she did, how well could she follow it? He felt more and more helpless as he looked. It was incredibly rough country. He wasn't sure if even Jim had ever been through it — perhaps he'd flown over. It was hard for sheep to get into those mountains, and the food was so scarce there they rarely did. No one ever mustered those hills.

Billy kicked open the door, holding a load of firewood. Outside, the snow still fell silently. The dogs prowled by the open door, hungry.

'Dogs are hungry,' stated Billy, stacking the wood. 'Take this,' he said, handing the axe to Tod. 'Get us some tucker, an' one for the dogs, eh.'

Kill two sheep — it was what Jim did. He had *watched,* he knew *how* to do it, but it had always been one of his father's jobs. But now, out by the little mob in the gully, he stood unnerved; the sheep were so big. Would a single blow do it? What if he missed? The sheep, dazed, screaming in pain, thrashing . . .

Tod took a deep breath and looked for one to kill. That one, there — no, it was a ewe, and a young one. He searched frantically in the dim light. No, not a young ram. Here, here was one. An older wether. He lifted the axe, butt poised. The wether moved off, pawing at the grass under the snow to graze. Tod felt the sweat cooling under his jersey.

He moved forward, brought the axe butt down, felt it jar up his arms as it hit the wether's head. The sheep kicked once, dropped with a thud. Tod ripped at his belt, grabbing for his knife. He yanked back the head, sticking the knife deep into the throat. The cold air sobbed in his throat, and the sound he thought the sheep was making was his own. The blood almost hissed on the icy snow, blazing out on to the whiteness with a violence of red that shocked the boy into immobility. He stood stiff. Was *that* all there was to it; it was that easy?

He grabbed the hind legs of the animal and dragged it up towards the hut. Panting, he moved back towards the mob. The other sheep never stirred. He chose another. This time, he did miss as he had feared. He grabbed it as it ran in a dazed zig-zag. He lifted the heavy axe with one hand, trying to hold the sheep with another. He had to let it go.

This was dumb. Jim did this all the time. He chose his wether coldly, approached it, hit it, slit its throat. No problem, all smooth motion. He dragged it up next to the other, blood smoking against the snow.

From over the hill came the first sound of approaching men, and soon the place was alive with horses, barking dogs, the shouts of men greeting the warm hut and Billy. Tod ran a twine quickly around the hind legs so they could be dragged from horseback to the hut, and ran to greet the musterers and help them with their mob of sheep.

The blood had frozen and blackened his hands, tightening the skin, and he tried scraping it off with snow. Billy came towards him.

'Good job,' he said. Unexpectedly, the old man's praise warmed him. He smiled. That was good. That had been his father's job, always, and now *he* had done it.

'D'you think . . . do you reckon that's where she's gone? Up

99

there, I mean — to look for your otter?' Tod asked the question quickly, caught in the sudden warmth he felt for Billy, knowing he'd not have a chance again to discuss it with all the other men about.

'I reckon,' said Billy, his voice level. 'You figure you can find her.' It was not really a question.

'You think ... you think I should?' It was the first he had admitted to the plan forming in his mind. He felt his own certainty, but suddenly he wanted Billy to agree, to advise him. But the old man was knocking the snow off his boots against a rock, and walking towards the hut.

By noon, two more men had arrived with their sheep, and the snow still fell. The hut was heavy, smoky, warm with the sweat of men, the smell of drying clothes and leather. The dogs had formed their little hollows against the wall of the hut, and inside the men smoked and played cards, read year-old newspapers found in cracks by the bunks, or talked in contented, disjointed sentences. They were used to this sort of waiting, and came equipped with ancient, greasy decks of cards and if they could fit them in, old ragged books of undefined subject which they read seriously in the dim light.

Tod sat staring at his map. Even an invitation to the card game could not stir him.

'I *know* where she went! I know it!' he muttered glancing sideways at Billy sitting next to him. Billy did not answer. Tod sat silent another moment and finally shoved the map on to the old man's lap. Billy seemed preoccupied with rolling a cigarette.

'Look,' said Tod, in a low exasperated voice. 'Look how far it is — look where she had to go! It'd take *days* for them to think of going there — I reckon maybe they won't even *think* of it! An' I can't reach anybody on the radio.'

This time Billy paused, and looked at the map. He grunted.

'She'll stay put, wherever she is. They'll find her,' he said finally.

'But it could take days! She must have left before it snowed!'

'You got to trust her; she knows what she's doing,' said

100

Billy in his expressionless voice. His answer took Tod aback. It was as if the old man didn't want her to be found — as if he'd helped her to go! The boy sat back on his heels. He couldn't just sit here, knowing, *thinking* he knew, where she was.

With good sense, good planning, he knew he could ride out alone, look for her. He'd take food, a radio, plan a route and stick to it, leaving a plan of it with Billy . . . within a day, perhaps, help could be on its way. But Jim had told him to stay with the men . . .

'You think I ought to go?' he asked Billy, for the second time. Why wouldn't Billy just say: yes or no?

'You doing this for her or you?' said Billy, setting up some cards for a game of solitaire. The question hit the boy hard, and he stared at the floor.

Sure. He was going out to rescue his sister. Alexa. He thought of her, then imagined her, strong and lean and easy on the horse, calm, having planned all this — for he knew then that she'd done this deliberately, not on a whim. She had to have crossed the Waiau. She was riding where he had never been, or Jim either. She'd be in the storm, alone. He'd never done that . . .'

'Both,' he whispered at last. The old man slapped down a card, won his game, looked at Tod with satisfaction.

'Well. That's OK. You know . . . that's OK then,' he said. He folded his hands on his stomach, leaned back, and fell asleep. What did that mean, thought Tod in exasperation. He *knew*? Knew what? That he was going, he wanted to go, because he wanted to do what Alexa was doing? Because it was a challenge to him? He sighed, confused. Who cared what the reason was! He was going to find her!

He helped prepare a lunch of cold mutton and white bread for the men. They opened a tin of plums. The billy steamed on the fire. Outside, the snow sifted against the windows. Once again, he thought of Alexa out there, and it frightened him in a worrying way, partly he was worried for her, partly it was that she was doing something bigger, more dangerous, than he'd ever dreamed of . . .

101

'I'm going to find her,' he announced to the sleeping form of Billy. The old man opened his eyes. He saw the boy standing before him, defiant, frightened, daring him to, maybe *hoping* he would forbid him. Well, he couldn't hold back a storm; the boy had to go, just as Alexa had.

'Get the map,' he answered. Tod scrambled to his bunk, grabbed the map.

'She won't want you there,' the old man stated, suddenly. Tod looked at him blankly.

'Why?'

'Just so you know, mate — she won't want you there, when you find her.' Billy would say no more, but he helped Tod get the gear he would need. By unspoken agreement, they did not speak to the other men of Tod's plan although it was obvious in the small hut that Tod was about to leave. They packed a good-sized pack for the packhorse to carry, a rifle, a walkie-talkie, extra batteries, blankets, food.

'Take a dog,' Billy said. Tod was relieved and grateful. Asking for a dog would be too much, for they were needed on the muster. Maybe it meant that Billy approved. He looked at the old man, but could see no change on the flat face. He felt bursting with questions: why had he said Alexa would not want him to find her? But time was critical, and if he did not start out soon, the day would be too far gone to begin, and he would have to wait.

Billy smoothed out the map and sat eyeing it. He muttered something under his breath, and to Tod it sounded like: 'The new net goes fishing . . .'

'What do you mean?' asked Tod. Everything Billy said seemed to jangle in him, to disquiet him. He was strained with doubts over his decision, yet nothing could keep him now from riding out into the storm. He wondered vaguely why Billy did not forbid him; it would be reasonable. . .

'Comes a time, the kids test out how strong they are, how far they can go . . . sometimes they catch a lot of fish. Sometimes they catch nothing at all,' grinned Billy.

Was he talking about him or Alexa? Or what? Unsure, he watched Billy's face, to see what would happen next.

'But it's a poor man who hangs his new nets near him to admire, but never lets them out into the river for fear they will tear and break,' continued Billy, but he was mumbling to himself now.

They loaded the pack horse and fastened the saddle on Nelson. Tod chose Rose to come with him, feeling guilty. She was a valuable dog on the muster, better than Fleet, but he felt safe with her. She was so much Jim's dog; it was as if a little bit of his father were with him. She loped about in the snow, sensing the tenseness, eager.

'Billy,' said Tod, before he mounted up. The old man paused straightening the bridle straps. 'I just . . . I mean, you know why I have to go, don't you? I *can't* just sit around, even if Dad said I should. The thing is, I *know* where she is!' It was that last that bound him to his decision, finally. *Knowing* where she was. It excited, frightened, challenged him. It was as if she, or something, were daring him.

Billy put his veined, brown hand on the boy's shoulder. He had never done that before.

'I reckon I do,' he answered softly. Tod gazed at him. Billy hoisted him into the saddle, giving him last minute instructions on the radio, going over the arranged contact-times.

Then, 'You'll find her,' he said, suddenly. 'You're a good man. You got a good horse, eh, and a good dog. No one needs more!'

A good man. He'd called him a good *man*. The horse plunged off through the snow, and Tod felt strong in the saddle.

He rode down the narrow gully, where the snow had blown clear in patches and drifts piled along the slopes. Nelson picked his way carefully through icy rocks, and Rose padded silently behind. For an hour or more, it was slow, tedious riding. Just before he turned out of the gully he ran into the last two musterers straggling in with their mob of about forty sheep. Their dogs were quiet and tired, the sheep struggling through the drifts. The men rode horses with heads hung low in the cutting wind. Tod saw Hiwi and called out to him.

'Hey, mate!' the boy cried back to him. Tod grinned. That was the way it should be, someone calling him 'mate'. He felt warm and happy as Hiwi and the other man rode up.

'What're you doin' out here, eh!' cried Hiwi. 'What a bloody hell of a time *we've* had! Hope you've got us a good billy on!'

Tod hesitated before answering. Anyone would think what he was doing daft. He spoke slowly.

'I'm going to find my sister,' he said at last.

Hiwi grinned openly in admiration. 'Good on you!' he cried. 'I'd do the same, eh, if't were me.' He turned and glared after the other man who was still making his way steadily with the mob towards the hut. 'Tell you what — I've had enough of this bloody job: I'll come with you, I will!'

Tod struggled with an answer, torn. He wanted his friend with him. But he needed to do this thing alone. He didn't realise that Hiwi was joking with him.

'I don't know — I think I got to go by myself,' he said in a low voice. Hiwi laughed out loud.

'You think *I'm* daft?' he said, 'You got to go; she's your sister. *I'll* stay home an' keep the billy warm for you, eh!' Tod relaxed, they laughed, and Hiwi turned his tired horse after the mob, waving without looking back.

Tod called Billy on the walkie-talkie before moving out of the gorge.

'Reckon it'll take me three hours to get up to the hut on Black Spur. Call you then. Over.' The little receiver crackled violently with interference, and he couldn't make out Billy's reply. He turned Nelson up the slope, out of the semi-protected gully and into the open hills of the high tussock ranges.

The snow let up at last during the afternoon. It was impossible to figure out how much time he was taking. He rode slowly, carefully, saving the horses. The land got steadily higher, colder, more barren. He stopped frequently to study the map at first, until he was certain he was heading in the right direction. He weighed the choices of where to ride: along this ridge, where it might be more windswept and free of snow, or the shorter way through this ravine, where each step would be in three foot drifts? He was startled from his thoughts by Rose's eager bark.

She had something bailed up in a thick grove of matagouri. Tod rode in and saw a herd of goats that had taken shelter there during the storm. They stood facing the dog. Automatically, he slipped his rifle out, flicking the catch.

The huge billy goat stood facing him. His massive coat of long tangled fleece hung gold and black to the snow, crusted with ice. His great segmented horns curved strongly back over his thick neck, curling around over his ears. The wild yellow eyes flecked with bronze and black glared at him. Around him stood the other goats, browns and golds and ochres and blonds, long fleeces whipping back in the wind. They were so wild, so beautiful; Tod lowered the rifle, called softly to Rose. Somehow, he found he could not feel like a farmer today. Today, the station belonged to no one; it was a wild place, full of wind and hidden life, and he was in it equal with the goats and deer and great green parrots of the icy slopes.

Tod thought of Alexa making her way through this land alone. He felt a thrill of love and a thrill of fierce fright. Somehow, she had passed him by, gone beyond him to a place he couldn't understand. He felt dull, slow. That was what Billy had meant! This was *her* path he was taking; it was her journey, just as the muster had been his — and she hadn't been allowed on the muster. He shook his head wildly. Such thoughts! He smiled nervously to himself. The kid was lost; he knew where she was. She had to be found — that was it.

At the top of a spur he turned and scanned the unreal landscape spiralling out around him. It was another world, a moon-world, all grey and white and black, mountain and hill jabbing into sky, marching forever into the grey-white sky, and beyond them, the vast realm of the king-like Kaikouras that reached to the edge of the sea. Could he really find her, in all this?

He trusted the map; it felt warm and comforting in the pocket against his chest. He followed a small river for a while, where the ground was flat. The soft mud on the banks was frozen solid and Nelson had some relief from the constant unevenness of the ground under the snow. When he turned the horse at last away from the river to start the last steep climb towards the hills of Black Spur, the tussock got thicker, spikier. The thorns on the matagouri raked at the horse's belly, tore at Tod's legs. At times, he had to hitch his legs up on the saddle to avoid being torn to shreds. Rose yelped softly.

He looked back and saw her gnawing at her foot. He slid off the horse and ran back. A thorn was wedged in Rose's foot. He pulled it out with his pliers, holding his breath to steady his hand. A thorn broken off in a dog's foot could be disastrous. Rose stood and licked her paw and in a moment she was fine.

Tod was anxious now. Was he as close to the hut as the map seemed to show? Estimations from map to the landscape could be inaccurate, and that would be fatal. He didn't allow himself the thought of what it would be like to be caught out here at night, with no way to follow landmarks. By the time he reached the edge of a huge beech forest which covered the slopes of several hills in front of him, it was dusk. The snow had started again; he realised he didn't know how long ago it had started.

It was so dark he didn't see the little hut until he was a few metres away, and if he had not been staring into the forest he might have ridden right past it. The hut backed into the bush, blending into the darkness. He stopped, his stomach folding inside him. How dark the hut was, the windows staring blackly at him, the tin dull and cold in the late dusk! Before he went in, he gathered dead wood from the edge of the bush. The trees loomed around him. He spoke roughly, loudly, to Rose, keeping her next to him, leading the horses along even as he picked up sticks.

When he had a fire burning in the open-brick pit inside the hut, Tod felt better. He had Rose with him, and resisted the ridiculous impulse to lead the horses in as well. He made himself some tea, ate some cold mutton and bread and some of the precious chocolate. He threw his cold bedroll on to the bunk nearest the fire and pulled off his boots and jerseys. The hut was cold everywhere but the tiny area around the fire. The flames danced on the dark walls and he felt comforted. His sleeping bag was warm when he climbed inside.

Sometime during the night he woke up. The fire had died to a deep glow in the blackness of the hut. He didn't know what had woken him. Had the wind got fiercer? Had the snow cracked a tree under its weight? He lay stiff in the cold. Rose crawled on to the bunk with him, and he slept.

9

HER FIRE HAD long since gone out. It was the dead heaviness of cold that woke her. Alexa curled into a tight ball, cramming the blankets under her. Something was missing. Max. He had left the cave, and she needed his warmth. She pulled each limb out separately, feeling no sensation in her legs and feet. Panic hit her with a blow like a sledgehammer. She jumped up, hit her head on the low roof of the cave, cried out. The air in the cave felt dead to her; she needed to breathe. She crawled out.

There was no world. There was only swirling, silent whiteness. Alexa stood rooted, unable to make her body move. Where was the lake, the mountains? Where was the magical, forgotten valley of yesterday? There was nothing here! Just cold and snow and the shadows of black rock. What could she do now?

Still she stood, unmoving, until the reality of being totally alone slammed into her. Max. Where was Max? She screamed his name, suddenly, and the sound cut through the whiteness and was absorbed by it. The silence which followed was even more terrible. It shook loose her legs, her body and she threw herself forward through the snow, running to the beach, not seeing the lake. She turned again, stumbling through a drift and ran toward the rock-slide. Max! Max! Where was he? She could not bear this, without the dog.

She ran up the shoreline. Her feet felt nothing on the rocks. When she got to a jumble of fallen boulders, she scrabbled over them. She had to use her hands to pull up her legs; they would not lift themselves. She grasped the stiff cloth of her pants, pulled, dropped the leg. Her foot hit the ground with a thud and she felt nothing. Panting, she leaned helpless on the grey stone.

This was no good. She bashed her leg against a rock, screaming at it. Bloody feet! Bloody feet! Move! She jumped up against the rocks, sliding down, unable to grasp the slippery surface. She pounded her feet with her fists, struggled up, thumped in the snow with them. Must look like a crazy person, she thought. Snow-crazy . . . Max! Max! Where are you! A crazy idiot dancing in the snow. She laughed shrilly. The cold seared her lungs, pulled her skin. She slowly slumped to the snow, curling herself into the rocks, watching fascinated as the snow sifted down, settled on her thighs, covering her coat. She curled tighter, grasping her feet with her hands. Yes, her feet were there. They were tricking her, pretending they weren't there so she couldn't feel them. Funny, how warm the rocks are. The snow was so warm. So tired. She was tired. I will sleep a little, and then Max will come, she thought. She closed her eyes.

A sharp stone hit Alexa's cheek. She brushed it away without opening her eyes. A moment, and another shower of gravel spattered against her. She stirred angrily. The cold crept in; she muttered and curled. The stones fell more insistently. She cried. She had to sit up. She looked around.

Above her on the rocks, sleek and lithe in the swirling snow, stood the otter. His body curved gracefully down as he watched her. The broad head was small and strong, the eyes so black they glinted. Muscles rippled under dark fur; the otter flattened against the rock. The slight movement sent another shower of pebbles down on the girl. She sat up.

They stared at each other. She felt the otter's body and self as if it were her own. She felt the blood in him pulsing through the graceful shape, felt his muscles flex and move under the skin. She felt the beautiful fur warm on him, felt the colour if it — rich brown on the back, fading to creamy-white on the belly. She felt it all through her own body, and still he stood above her on the rocks, intelligent eyes boring into her, sensitive nose fluttering to take in every part of her. She felt herself becoming full and warm and rich, felt the life stirring through her. She blinked. When she looked again, the rocks were bare, and the otter was gone. She stood up, ran her hand over the stone. It was damp, as if a creature had recently been there. She ran to the lake. The surface of the water rippled slightly and grew still.

And Max trotted down from the far end of the forest, a rabbit limp in his jaws. Alexa felt her face tighten in the cold as she smiled.

'Oh, Max!' she called him softly. The big dog came to her and dropped the rabbit. He pressed his great body against her legs. She hugged him. 'That's where you've been! You were hungry! I was so afraid, Max! All the time I forgot you were hungry, just like me!' She gave the rabbit back to him and went towards the cave.

She built up the fire again and got the remains of the eel from a hole in the rock. It was cold and stiff, the slime under its skin congealed to a white paste. She shoved a stick through it and thrust it into the flame. Max tore at the rabbit, eating everything but ears and tail. When she had eaten and warmed slightly, she took off her boots and examined her feet. It had been stupid to sleep the night before with the boots on. She forced herself to consider the possibility of frostbite, and massaged the toes vigorously. Her feet were dead white, but she could see no dangerous shots of red under the skin. She pushed them as close to the fire as she dared and continued rubbing them. At first it brought only a tingle, but as she worked, the pain came and shot through her until she squirmed on the cold sand. She kept rubbing mechanically. As the blood returned it made her legs jerk with pain, but she knew then that they would be all right.

At last she was able to sit quietly, her feet warm and still tingling slightly, the cave warmed a bit, the flames dancing red and hot on the walls of rock and Max lying beside her, his own hunger calmed. She found if she spoke aloud, her thoughts came clearer, her fear lessened. The dog lay and listened.

'I can't do that again,' she scolded herself. For the first time, she thought of the otter who had forced her out of her deadly, exhausted sleep. He had known that what would kill her quickest would be her own panic. He had pulled her out of it. Why?

And how had he known?

'It's as if . . .he isn't really an animal,' she whispered to the dog. She could hear the words of her story, she could hear Billy's voice telling her, and she knew why it had stayed with her. The essence of the otter had come through to her, something timeless and magic, secret, something which lured her with its promise. It promised she would *know* things, know important things — answers she didn't even have questions to yet. And Billy had recognised her need for that promise.

'I don't even know if he's real,' she continued. The words were soft in the rocks. 'How could he have known I would die if I'd kept on sleeping? And how did he know I needed food, last night?' She found she was swaying slightly with the rhythm of her own questions. And it came to her then that it did not even matter. It did not matter if the otter were real. He lived in the lake, and came out of the water to her, and that was real enough. The tough black skin of the eel lay charred in the ashes: that was real. The tiny scratch on her face where one of the sharper stones had hit as she slept: that was real, too. And no one ever had to know about any of this. Inside her, it was real. Just like inside Billy, it was real. People thought his stories were just stories, but that did not matter because Billy kept them real inside. And she knew why he told them, then. Because maybe, once, just once, someone would hear one and take it for their own and keep it inside like he did, and maybe they would take that story with them on a journey to find its very beginning. And giving the story to someone else was the most important thing of all.

Alexa straightened the moss inside the cave. She threw out

111

the remains of the rabbit and the eel. It was still snowing outside. She remembered with a guilty start that she had forgotten all about Hobo, so she ran out to the tea tree to look for him. He hobbled out of the trees slowly, head down. She let him loose so he could graze and he wandered off. He still limped badly and she saw he could not stand on his bad foot and paw through the snow for food with his other. So she gathered armfuls of tussock for him, cutting it with her kitchen knife. She realised he would not survive another night unless she could keep him warmer. The blankets would keep the wind out, and together with the trees, Hobo could survive the cold. But she had to have the blankets herself.

Hunger turned her thoughts away from the horse. The snow fell softly and steadily in small, wind-whirled flakes, in a way that seemed it would never stop. She was able to see around her more clearly than she had in her panic that morning. Her mountain-locked valley was completely white. The great rocks that were not yet covered were black and grey softened by mantles of white. Ochre tussock still poked through. The lake was flat, depthless, lead-grey. She thought of the eel, and knew there would be more hidden in the weeds at the water's edge. It took too long and yielded too little to search for *koura* again.

Alexa had never caught eel before, but she knew they were fast and could bite if they weren't held correctly. Tod used to bring them home triumphantly. She squeezed her eyes shut to remember if he'd ever described catching them. Had they been caught on a line? She didn't have anything for a line, or bait either. Spearing? She could fasten the knife on the end of a stick . . .

As she stood pondering, there was a great screeching and clattering of wings and three keas flew down from high up a rocky cliff. She grinned, delighted. They were such cheeky, bright creatures; she was glad they'd come. With a spatter of orange and red feathers the keas landed in a dense thicket of scrub, calling and diving in the branches. When they landed on the snow to dig into the tussock, their green feathers were brilliant against the whiteness and when they lifted their tails, the colour was breathtaking.

One kea flashed up again, disappearing deep into the bush. She could hear him chortling and cackling to himself as he scuttled about in the branches. It made her laugh aloud. In another moment he was out again, with a triumphant screech, dragging something in his beak. She watched him grasp it in his claws, dip his head to strip the berries from the branch he'd found. She took a step nearer. It was a branch from a snowberry bush! Against the snow, the bright fat berries seemed to glow, matching the greedy glow in the kea's eyes as he plucked the berries. Of course! She had forgotten all about snowberries. The fruit would be perfectly ripe now, sweet and full. She fought her way into the thicket, going in the direction she thought the kea had been. There was a whole patch of the little bushes, their thorny twigs laden with berries. She thought she'd never seen anything as lovely as those dark red berries on the black twigs, each berry capped with white, each twig lined with white. She filled her pockets, then, braving the wind, took off her jacket and piled berries in it till she had stripped the bush. She felt like screeching in triumph herself as she pushed her way slowly back.

She scooped a hole in the sand in the cave and dumped the berries in it. Shivering, she put her jacket back on and wrapped a blanket around herself until she had warmed a bit. She thought of the coming night, and Hobo . . .

But the berries would not be enough, or last long. She still needed more. She was drawn to the lake as much for the presence of the otter as because it held food for her. She took her knife and set out.

Eels would most likely be where there was an abundance of weed, and at her part of the lake, the shoreline was clean and sandy, but in places, ice had formed and the going was slippery. Streams thundered down into the lake, scudding and leaping down the cracks and fissures of rock from unbelievable heights. She moved carefully, the fear for her feet from that morning's panic still deep in her. If she got frostbite, that was it. Above her, the great mountain walls towered, muffled with snow. Everywhere was the sound of the mountains, and she wondered why it had seemed so unbearably silent that morning. The fresh snow crackled in the beech trees, snapping branches with a rifle-shot crack. From all around came the low rumble of distant snow-slides, and she could see at times the puff of snow-smoke as a slab tumbled down the mountainside. Under her boots, ice snapped and rocks clattered. At one streamside she stopped. The water here was thick with weed. Sweet bright watercress grew in the stream itself. She gathered handfuls and piled it on the ground. She stared into the lake water now, clear as clear, choked with great thick plants. She would try here for eels. She knew they hid under overhangs and logs, so she took a stick and stirred the weeds on the surface. Very quickly, she found a submerged log propped on another further down. A perfect place. She poked under it fiercely, straining to see if anything moved.

There was a violent lashing under the water and an eel flew from the log and disappeared into the weeds. Alexa scrambled along the bank, excited. There it was, hiding its purple body muscled and curled in the murky weeds. Alexa held her breath, leaning forward, her feet clutching the very edge of the shore. Then she rolled her sleeve up, poised, shot out her arm, felt the ice of the water.

Something slammed with such force into her hand that she screamed and fell on to her knees in the water. She closed her hand convulsively around a smooth, slimy body, and felt herself jarred violently forward. Some will other than her own forced her to keep a hold of the lashing body of the eel. Her knees and elbows were now in the water. She wrenched herself back, grasping the writhing body of the eel with both hands. She dug her nails into the skin and stood up. Her arms were numb with cold but she managed to throw the eel on to the stones with all her force. It lay stunned. Only then did she see the blood on her hand and begin to feel the pain as the cold wore off. Alexa became angry. She did not know why — perhaps it was seeing the blood dripping on to the snow, seeing it was *her* blood, seeing the ugly, pulsing body of the eel flipping on the rocks where it lay stunned. She grabbed a stone and brought it down with a grunt on its angular head. As she stood staring down at the still-writhing body, the pain from the eel's bite shot through her. She clutched her hand and looked at it. The palm had a deep, ragged gash in it, which still bled. Her arm ran blood now, mixed with water. She plunged it again into the lake to clean it and dull the pain. When the bleeding stopped, she examined it. It was a deep bite, the skin punctured and torn unevenly.

Alexa ran back to the cave, dragging the eel through the snow. It was big, longer than her arm and as thick. She examined in fascination the rows of teeth, tiny and needle-sharp, in the mangled head. She tore off another strip from her precious blanket and wrapped her throbbing hand. She couldn't bring herself to think about the wound, for she could feel the onset of panic. Instead, she slit the eel lengthwise, cut through the backbone, and laid it skin-down on the stones. The fire had died to embers, but she started it up again, using the last of the dead branches she'd collected. Then, exhaustion and a numb mind overcoming her, she curled next to it, pulled the moss and blankets around her, and slept.

It was hard to tell the time of day when Alexa woke, but she imagined she had slept for several hours. It might be mid-afternoon. The snow had stopped and the air had cleared. Something had startled her awake. She climbed out, stood listening. There. Again. From far off, the unmistakable bark of Max rang out over the water. Had he gone off hunting again? This bark was the bark of a dog who had something bailed up. It was the bark of a huntaway keeping things in order. She could tell it came from one place and did not move, and it sounded calm and steady. What could he have found?

Alexa felt strong after her sleep. Her hand hurt her, but when she pulled off the blanket, she saw it was not swollen. She cradled it against her as she followed the sound of Max's barking.

He was closer than she thought, just past the swamp and somewhere up the slope of a beech forest. The sound of his bark echoed out over the water, hitting the far mountains, bouncing around, confusing her. She called him, then waited, tense, hearing a crashing in the undergrowth. At last the dog dashed out to her, stood a second, and ran back up the slope. She followed into the forest, tripping on vines, panting, struggling for balance with her one good hand. The snow had sifted down through the branches and lay softly on everything. The forest looked lighter with its covering of snow, and not so eerie.

Max stood, not barking now, under a shelf of rock jutting out from the slope. Above him, on the ledge, three goats stood, braced to run, yet strangely hesitant. She didn't see the fourth goat for a moment, but when she did, she knew he was the reason the others stayed. Lying on his side in the snow in a tangle of creepers lay a big goat. She could see he was magnificent, with a pitch black coat of fur, tangled and matted in the snow. His horns had scored deep cuts in the snow and into the soft loam below. He could see her, and he lay quiet, wanting to move, but helpless, glaring at her. Around him on low branches sat some keas, and from farther off, she could see even a falcon had penetrated the dense branches following the promise of a good feed. For a moment, there was no movement.

Alexa moved forward, curious. The goat was injured, but how? She could see no wound, and he looked a strong young billy. His mouth was open and his tongue protruded slightly as he panted. She stared at the graceful head, the round gold eyes. When she moved forward again, the goat thrashed suddenly, wildly, bleating, and struggled to his feet. He stood splay-legged and lowered his head, swinging the heavy horns. She stepped back rapidly, tripping on a log and landed heavily on her back where she lay without moving. The goat squealed and she could see he was in some great pain. His legs buckled, and he crashed down again into the snow, then lay still again, his sides rising and falling with laboured breath. Max circled warily. The keas shifted on the branches.

The falcon circled silently and descended closer. Alexa knew they would land soon. She'd had her knife when she

116

came out of the cave, but now it was not in her belt. She crawled back, on her belly, searching for it. When she looked again, the keas had descended already, hopping over the thick neck, peering into the wild face. The golden eyes of the goat blinked, once. When the falcon dropped down, the keas flew at him, beaks open, head feathers erect. The falcon hissed, struck out. The keas crashed up into the low branches, screeching. Almost with dignity, the hawk stepped on to the head, lowered his beak.

Alexa threw herself forward. She dashed in, waving her hands. The goat still panted, but could no longer struggle. He moved his legs, the sharp hooves cutting into the earth.

She caught the glint of metal in the leaves just under the rock; it was her knife, where it had fallen when she tripped. She picked it up, felt its weight in her hand. She had never killed anything like this, nothing so *big,* so wild and beautiful. It was thrashing again, struggling to the last. But the keas would peck out the eyes first, while the beast writhed beneath them. And then the falcon, with his rapier beak, tearing into the soft underbelly still pumping blood — she shuddered, swallowed. She had to kill it. She couldn't leave it like this.

She approached warily. Her arm felt weak, and her hand with the bite hurt. She willed herself to calm. She studied the animal. He was immense, much larger than a domestic goat. His horns could break her leg, if they caught her as he thrashed his head. She pointed the blade. What if I miss? The breath caught in her throat. What if he doesn't die straight away?

Nevertheless she jumped in, plunged the blade down. The blade hitting the flesh jarred her arm, sending shock through her. Blood shot into the air, and she knew she'd hit the jugular. The goat kicked twice, and the sharp hooves caught her on the shin and sent her sprawling again. But the goat was dead. The keas flew in at once, squabbling over the head. She screamed at them.

Her hand and now her leg throbbed dully. She knelt and felt the fur, ran her hand over the smooth face, feeling the

117

delicate lines from eye to muzzle. The fur felt like velvet. She ran her hand up the horns; they were hot to the touch and that surprised her. They had smooth ridges on them. Alexa inspected the goat more carefully now, trying to find the reason for his strange behaviour. He was thin under all the fur, but he was young. Suddenly she remembered the other three and turned to look, but they must have fled. Perhaps he had been the leader of the group. She tried to feel under him, and up on his neck, underneath, she suddenly felt a lump. She struggled to pull the head around, to discover what it was.

There was a wound high on the neck; when she finally could see it, she saw it had been deeply infected, as if it were very old, and he had carried it around for some time. She probed at the festered skin with her knife, pulling away the matted fur. There was something hard in there: a bullet from a high-powered rifle. It had lodged in his neck, working its way slowly in, festering, until finally it struck a nerve, or the infection poisoned him and he had been able to go no further.

He no longer looked to her so perfect and so wild. He lay black and bloody on the snow. The sight of the bullet wound had sickened her, in a way she could not understand: she'd seen wounds before, after all. But this wound was an intrusion of the outside world. The whole animal made her feel sick. She wished she'd just left him where she'd found him.

As Alexa looked down at the dead goat, she found herself staring at the strands of thick fur spread over the snow. Nothing could penetrate that coat; it could have survived any winter up here in the mountains. That coat — if she could only have it! Hobo could have the blankets, and they would both survive the nights ahead!

She pulled at the carcass, already stiffening in the cold. How to begin — she tried to remember her father, skinning a sheep. Cut around the neck, the legs, slit the belly up . . .

She thrust the knife into the soft skin of the abdomen and worked in under up to the neck. She slit the legs raggedly, the carcass was already turning stiff under her, but she sawed through the thick pelt to cut the skin from the neck. The goat was much heavier than she could lift, but she struggled to drag it over. The blood on her hands congealed to heavy coldness, making it hard to manipulate the knife. Bracing herself against a rock, she tugged at the stiff, slippery mass of bloody skin and tangled hair. It came slowly, a bit at a time. When at last it pulled free, covered with blood and dirty snow and leaves, she rolled it up and clasped it to her. If she didn't scrape it soon, it would dry and freeze stiff as a board, and be of no use. Her breath rang in her throat. Max sniffed at the carcass, and she realised that here was food for the dog for many days. The meat might be too strong for her to eat, even as hungry as she could get. But she hacked at the animal anyway, sawing a few chunks of haunch meat to take with her. The cloying smell of thickening blood rose like steam in the cold still air, and she felt sick again.

Alexa spread the pelt as best she could on a flat boulder, skin side up. It was hard to hold it and scrape at the same time, and the blade of the kitchen knife was almost useless for the task. She sat back exhausted, on her heels.

At the lakeside, the water stirred and broke. Her breath caught in her throat with joy. When the otter appeared, it was like a message of strength. She wondered why he had never shown any fear of her. The otter slid from the water, climbing through the thin ice on the shore so it fell tinkling into the water. Then the water stirred again and Alexa gasped aloud as a second otter bounded on to the sand! For a moment, the two animals watched her, balanced on their strong hind feet and broad thick tails. The creamy fur on their bellies gleamed in the white light of the afternoon. She could see their black eyes glittering, and saw the thick whiskers twitching constantly, the tiny close ears move slightly. Alexa felt every sense of her own sharpened and she wondered if that was what it was to be an animal, a wild animal, perfect in its world: to feel every stir of air on her skin, to feel every scent in her nostrils, to feel every minute roughness of rock under her fingertips. She was suddenly aware of every heartbeat of hers, and of each course of blood through the veins of her body; she could feel each toe, each finger, each leg and arm. It was as if her whole being had been opened up, exposed, and all of her streamed out, was touched, touched, and coursed back in through all the pores of her skin, through every sense she had. Was that what it was to be an otter? Was that what Max, the keas, even old Hobo, felt? She felt drunk, giddy, exhilarated. When the otters ran through the rocks, playing and leaping, folding into one another, sliding through weeds, disappearing, reappearing in the dark water, Alexa felt her own body with theirs. No! This was not just being an animal! This was what it was to be ALIVE! This was what it was to *know*, to know you were alive, to know you were in the world, with the world around you and in you, and to know you could move perfectly and beautifully through it all. She leapt up, the knife clattering beside her on the stones. She ran towards them, and they did not go, but kept only just ahead of her, out of reach, playing, chittering, chirring softly, slipping in and out of the water. She ran with them until she was exhausted. And when the sound of the plane came to them off the echoing slopes of the mountains, the whole world stopped.

The otters were gone before Alexa could take in her breath. The lake closed over them without a trace. And with her second breath, she too dived into the forest behind her, calling Max, crouching tensed under the dark creepers in the wet snow. How long she knelt in the snow there she didn't know. It seemed the mountains held the sound of the plane forever, its whine and dull roar bounding from cliff to cliff, rock-slide to fissure. It sliced through her heightened senses like a burning poker through her body; she squeezed her mind shut against the sound, trying to squeeze shut her senses. Long after the echoes died away over the ridgetops she knelt there, shattered. When at last the cold stole past her defences, she found she was crying; she crashed through the forest's edge on to the shore, gasping, sobbing, the tears freezing on her cheeks. She stood staring up at the dark ridges surrounding her hidden valley. The sky was steel grey and all was silent.

Why? What had she run for? That was a search plane: it had been looking for her! Why had she run? She had reacted instinctively, as the otters had, as a wild thing. She had run and hidden. And now the plane, maybe her only chance of being rescued, was gone.

Rescued? She sat heavily on the rock. Don't I want to be rescued? She wondered. Her thoughts returned to her now, and she felt calm, amazed. Max stole up beside her, leaning his head against her.

'I'm not ready yet,' she whispered. She thought, I'm close to something. I almost *know* something. Maybe I almost know why I came!

That moment on the beach as she had sat watching the two otters, when all of her had opened to the whole world, seemed the edge of a secret, the edge of *knowing* something important and secret. And it had lasted only a fraction of a minute. It was still tender and unformed, that *knowing*. She could lose it, and once she lost it, it might never come to her again. Perhaps the otters would never come again! That was why she had run. She nodded her head. That was why. She had been in the middle of an important discovery, and something had interrupted her.

When I know why I came here, she thought to herself, that's when I'll go back. And I *almost* knew, when the otters were here. I almost knew! She smiled, and picked up her knife, and turned to finish her task of scraping the goat pelt.

121

10

TOD RODE AS if asleep. For hours he had been pushing Nelson through the drifts, steadily; since morning when he had left the little hut in the forest, it had snowed lightly, in a mist of flakes. It was an eerie and strange landscape he rode through. The hills ran like fingers, spurs and gullies, deep ravines and scree-covered slopes, mountains and saddles, all covered with the hypnotic glare of white. In places, the snow had been swept clear by the wind, and a patch of tussock showed, or a pile of rocks.

Tod stopped constantly to check his position against the map and compass. The detours caused by drifts of snow threw him off course sometimes for an hour or more. Nelson picked his way surely, seeming to sense the deep pockets and drifts, able to move through spikes of spaniard grass and the thorns of matagouri which lay, as menacing as icebergs, just under the drifts with only the tips of the bush showing. Often, Tod walked behind the horse, giving directions with his voice or a light touch of his hand. He spoke often, needing to hear his voice in the soft muffled infinite landscape.

What would Alexa be doing out there? In his thoughts he imagined her at the little lake he could see on the map. Something in him felt sure, felt convinced she was there. But his nagging doubts still caused him to question: had she survived the snow? Had she been able to follow her map — he'd only just showed her how to read it.

He thought about Billy's words. Otters. Who on earth would think an otter could exist in a tiny lake in the high country of the South Island? Yet it had a strangely alluring image: a warm-blooded, graceful animal living secretly in lakes so high that very few forms of life could be found in them. He began to see why Alexa had found it so compelling she had to search for it. After all, didn't he feel compelled to search for *her*? Wasn't he just as sure she was there as she must have been sure about her otter?

He hugged his arms about himself and snorted. The snow was making him have crazy thoughts! He stopped Nelson again, studying the map. Damn! He'd been thrown off his route again by having to traverse that gorge too choked with snow for the horse to get through. He'd have to double back, hit the other side of that spur there . . .

For an hour or so he moved steadily on, Rose following in the track made by the horses. He found his thoughts turning again to Alexa, to Billy. The new net goes fishing, Billy had said. He, Tod, must be the new net, then. Alexa had already gone out, struck out on her own; she'd always been that way, he knew. Never needed permission, or approval, as he did. Just decided something, and then did it. She was always noticing things he did not — a tiny lizard half-hidden on a rock, a new-born lamb crouched on the tussock hills, a buck deer standing still as rock. And she'd show him. It was why he'd liked riding with her. He looked around him now from Nelson's back as they topped a low saddle. It seemed so barren and empty in the snow. It comforted him to see a few straggles of sheep out there. That was Jim's touch on the land; this was Jim's world, and now it was his. Jim filled the emptiness, gave it meaning.

By late afternoon the hills had grown into mountains and the going was excruciatingly slow. Tod could see he would never make it to the lake by the day's end. The idea of having to build a shelter for himself out of the snow worried him slightly, but he had been on short tramping expeditions with friends as a boy and had done it before. With common sense he would be fine.

The snow had stopped at midday, and now as he climbed a steep slope, he felt a damp warmish wind blowing down on him. If it snowed again, it would be wet. He hoped it would not rain. He looked at the ridge above him. Soft warm snow was dangerous — but he could see no other way to cross. On the map, he could see there was a small river ahead of him, with patches of beech forest. It would be where he could spend the night, as it would be warmer there, and out of the wind. But he had to reach it before dusk, for he had a lot of preparation to do before he could settle for the night. And there was this range to cross before he got there.

He urged Nelson through the snow and low scrub. By the time the scrub thinned and the slope became steeper his own legs were scratched and burning from the rough bark and thorns. He gave Nelson free rein. Wind had cleared this slope in many places and the loose shale and rock showed through. Nelson would have to pick his way on his own.

When they reached the saddle, he stopped to take his bearings. A light sprinkling of snow had started again, driven in on the wind. Below him the ridge fell sharply to a ledge-like drop, then fell again into a shallow, beech-filled gorge. Through the gorge a small, white frothing river ran, twisting through rocks and overhanging trees. A low bank ran along the far shore, and a narrow band of tussock ran into a scrub forest of manuka and wind-dwarfed trees. And beyond that, and above it, was a wall of mountains which stretched forever beyond his sight. They rose black and snow-slashed from the little gorge, towering in jagged layers, higher and higher, at times hidden in mists, at times falling to sweeping saddles cutting the edge of sky. He studied his map. It was over those mountains he would find the lake.

Tod's heart lurched and sank. How could Alexa have traversed those mighty walls of stone and snow? How could that old Hobo have made his way up there? Even if they had come at it from another direction, as he thought they must have, the mountains would still (he could see from the map) have been as forbidding, as terrible. Somewhere within those heights was a lake so tiny, so perfect, like an oval gem of unearthly blue, and she had searched for it. Had she found it?

With a start, Tod came back to where he was, and saw that it was near dusk already. He quelled the urge to hurry, knowing that would be foolhardy. He untied the packhorse from Nelson's saddle, dismounted, and started slowly down the snow-covered slope. Here the snow had blown into great drifts in places. Rose once sank out of sight, and Tod stumbled occasionally in thigh-deep snow. Nelson and the packhorse slid on their haunches, scrabbling for a foothold, crashing through the crust. The wind shifted suddenly, coming full at them, blowing great clouds of loose snow up in little whirlwinds. Tod stuck his face into his coat and felt his way down blindly, unable to see horses or even Rose. They were on their own.

There was a low roar behind him and he thought it was the wind increasing its velocity. But then Nelson's shrill whinney cut across the sound. He looked back. The snow moved under his feet, shifting sluggishly, as if something was emerging from beneath it after a long sleep. The mountain rumbled. Through the wind-whipped snow clouds, he saw the slope behind him move; the whiteness became alive, slipping towards him, gaining speed. The roar entered him like a scream, and he was screaming, lost his feet, flung himself forward.

It was only a small avalanche, and the steepness of the slope helped him. He lost footing and fell, willing his knees to lock, to hold him, to push him forward . . . Around him the snow smoked and belched and roared, and still he pushed himself down, his breath tearing at his throat.

He hit full length a cropping of rocks, and dropped solidly from them on to a ledge below. He lay stunned, his breath drowning in his chest. When at last he could breathe, Tod found the roaring was now only in his head, and around him the mountain was still again. The ground lay solid and still under his feet. Tod pulled himself up and looked back. The scar where the snow had broken away above him looked small, like a tiny cut. Below him, in a gully, the fallen mass still smoked. His breathing slowed, became even again. I have survived an avalanche, he thought dumbly. He was all alone. There were no animals to be seen.

Rose. Rose. He plodded slowly towards the soft pile in the gully. Rose. He sunk to his waist in the soft snow, and stood there, numb. He'd lost Rose. And Nelson. And the packhorse, with the radio and all his supplies. A stirring in the scrub below him brought him out of his stupor.

'Rose?' he called, hardly daring to hope, then, 'Rose!' loudly and clearly; joyfully, he pounded down towards her. She emerged from the bushes, shook herself, barked. He threw himself on her. She stood and looked at him. Good old Rose. She came out of everything. She waited for him now, eager: what next? what do we do now?

He had little hope for the horses. He expected to find them twisted in the gully, perhaps a leg showing, or the tip of an ear, buried and broken under the snow. Yet he searched methodically, poking with a stick into the drifts.

Tod found the packhorse first; it had been thrown clear of the snow and lay on its side, still alive. Its hind legs were twisted under it. The horse struggled bravely, throwing out its front legs, heaving itself forward from its useless hind legs. The boy pulled the rifle from its case strapped on the packs and shot him. The shot cracked cleanly through the dim light, and the sound pierced deep into the boy's gut. He was crying now, cradling the dead horse's head in his arms. The soft velvet lips were drawn back over yellow teeth and he drew them down, covering them. He left him, and went for Nelson.

Perhaps he would have to shoot him, too. Alexa's horse, which he'd promised to look after. He should have turned back at that ridge, knowing the danger of soft snow. He should never have started this daft search, based on a whim. An otter, for God's sake! He should know that old man was crazy! And what made him think, just because she had looked at the map that night in the study, that she had gone to this god-forsaken lake in the back country where no one ever went? She could be anywhere; she could be buried under an avalanche, like Nelson. He cursed Billy, jabbing viciously

126

into the snow with his stick, tears choking him.

He didn't hear the soft whicker, at first. Only the prick of Rose's ears caught his attention, and then he heard it, too — an impatient, questioning nickering from somewhere below him. He stopped, stood unbelieving. How was this possible? He peered through the gathering darkness and saw the dark form of a horse standing at the bottom of the gully to his left. Nelson!

Tod scrambled down the slope and grabbed the huge head in his arms. Nelson butted at him, happily. He felt each leg carefully, felt the neck. He was all right. It was a miracle!

After transferring the dead horse's pack to Nelson, Tod moved into the forest that lined the river. It was dark, but the snow was not so deep. In the shelter of some rocks between the beeches, he made a tiny over-hang of dead branches and creepers cut with his hatchet, and covered this with his rolled-up tarpaulin. He scraped the snow out, laid a pile of spring vines and moss and covered it with blankets. Rose crawled in with him after he had tethered Nelson in the shelter of the trees, and exhausted, he fell into a deep sleep.

11

WHEN ALEXA CRAWLED from the cave on the morning of the fourth day, wrapped in the smelly goat pelt, she emerged into a world transformed into awesome brightness and beauty. Transfixed, she stood in the clear sharp sunlight, drinking in all she saw. Her tiny valley was no longer the kingdom of grey and rock and snow. The lake glistened in wavelets of silver light, and all around, the ice and snow reflected a million crystals of brilliance. The magic of her valley blinded her. She had accepted it as grey and black, as snow and whiteness and rock and cold. Now the snow sparkled with jewel-light, the moisture on the rocks frozen to a thin clear glaze, bringing out the greens of moss and lichen. The beech forest was hung with clusters of shining leaves, the tree trunks black and silver-lined. The dusky green of the manuka, the soft dun of tussock, the red of the snowberry capped in white, all glistening with ice, hung with icicles shimmering in the breeze. The lake, the lake! She couldn't believe the enchantment of the place. She ran to the water.

The otters were there already, waiting for her, playing with energy and abandon in the shallow waters of the edge. Their bodies glinted muscular and rich in the depthless blue of the lake, hardly stirring the surface. In the clear water, the bright green weed floated, and they played with it, with sticks, with little round pebbles. As they swam under the surface, the sun reached them and dappled their bodies through the swaying weeds.

'Kingdom of light,' she whispered to the lake. The words sounded solemn and religious. She felt religious, as if she were praying, or ought to be. Nothing could describe the feeling of being here, she thought. How could one describe feeling so — *part of* something as complete as this? The otters chirred happily on the rocks, and she sang back to them.

What a sight she must be! She stared down at herself, dirty pantlegs stuck out from under the massive, stiff, stinking pelt of goat fur, some of the hair trailing into the snow behind her. The sun made the air warmer, and she shrugged herself out from the black pelt. She ran to find Hobo. He stood wrapped in the blankets, warm and happy to see her. She led him out, let him free to graze the tussock beneath the shallow coating of snow. His leg was no longer swollen, but he only occasionally set it on the ground. He would not be able to be ridden for a long time. She stilled a whisper of worry intruding into the brilliance of the morning.

'Today is mine!' she cried. Max bounded beside her. She ignored the hunger gnawing at her. This would be a day to luxuriate in the valley's beauty, to be with the otters, to walk, to explore, to draw in her fat pad of paper, to think . . . She rejected the memories of yesterday's panics, the grubbing for survival, the eel bite, the bloody mess of the goat. She sang as she went back to the cave.

The sun had warmed the rocks so they were comfortable to sit on. Alexa opened her pad of paper on her knees and sat by the lake edge, watching the otters. From high up in the rocks on the cliffs around her some keas screeched, and she could see the brilliant orange feathers under their wings as they glided on the air currents from rock to rock above her. There was a clatter of rocks far, far off up the mountains, and she could just make out the forms of some large animals leaping from crag to ledge. Goats? She peered closer. No — they were chamois! Such rare, shy creatures: it made the valley all the more magic, hidden, secret. Her soft black pencil drew her world, drew the lithe otters, the dark-rimmed feathers of the kea, drew the horse grazing down the lake in the tussock.

Even then, she knew she could not keep them out forever. Even then, she began to admit them, hesitantly, one by one, first faces, then the names: Tod, Dad, Mum . . . Clive. She stopped her drawing, looked around. She was all alone and it was all perfect. But she knew it would end — not the valley, but her stay in it. She was overcome by an odd sensation, not quite sorrow, not quite fear — it came from knowing that she might never be able to speak of this place, for many reasons. There were practical, cold reasons: if others came, it would be spoiled, the animals would leave, the otters . . . She looked across to the water, where they played. Once again, she wondered if they were real.

Billy would say it didn't matter. Billy would tell her that the valley was a part of her, and that from then on, everything she said and did would come in part from the wild valley hidden in the mountains. Billy would say: every story you tell will have echoes of this place, and everything you see will be through your otter-eyes . . . How did she know, she wondered, what Billy would say? Had he already said it, and she'd forgotten? No. It had to be that she was only imagining him . . . but this comforted her. The loneliness that had hit her as she realised she could never directly speak of this place disappeared.

For a long time, the sun beat down into the valley, warming the girl as she sat drawing. The otters came and went. From deep within the beech-filled ravines cutting up the mountains, the liquid notes of the bell-bird came, or the scream of the kaka, half-hidden in its own echo. She could hear the crystallised crash of water from the tiny streams rushing into the ice-rimmed lake, and once in a while, the sharp crack of a slab of snow freed on the mountainside and roaring down in a puff of mist. And everywhere, under every stone and boulder, every log or fallen tree, came the steady soft drip-drip of melting ice, and the sparkle of bright water. Alexa, mesmerised, filled page after page of her little pad with drawings. Sometimes she drew what she saw — the otters, the mountains, the twisted beeches. And sometimes she drew what she felt inside her — faces, unrecognisable shapes, and sometimes words and bits of thought.

I will never leave here, she thought dreamily. I could just stay forever and ever . . . and she began to think how she could fix up her little cave, how she could find a regular source of food . . .

After a time, her thoughts returned to food more and more often and it came suddenly, like a rude visitor in this pristine world, that she was violently hungry. She tried to ignore it, but her drawings became smudgy, she felt restless on the stone, and finally she sighed and stood up. It was mid-morning and the sun filled the valley from the top of the sky.

She called Max and wandered lazily down the shore. She half-noticed that at a distance, and still playing, the otters were following. She headed toward the stream at the far end where she had found *koura* before, knowing that after several hours of searching she would have a good-sized meal. There had been watercress there, too. She rejected the idea of another eel — her hand still hurt from the nasty bite.

The magic of the valley had filled her so that all her movements felt dream-like and slow. Her hunger was like a tiny irritating mosquito buzzing about. Anything that threatened to disturb her sun-drenched contentment was annoying: hunger, and the persistent images of people from another time and place. She heard their voices too — Tod, calling her from across the yard, her mother speaking in low tones while the baby slept, and the full gruff voice of Jim speaking to the dogs . . . She heard Clive asking her to go to the pictures, and could not shake herself free of his strong-boned brown face looking down at her. And in and out of the sun-drenched trees, it seemed the voice and form of Billy came with her everywhere, following her like the otters followed her down the shoreline.

They have nothing to do with me here, she thought fiercely. This is my place, and I never felt that way before! I don't want them here!

But the form of Billy was in her eyes, and he was saying something to her softly, and she could not quite hear. The otters had dived deep into the black water shadowed by the forest and she could not see them surface. She peered over the water; they had disappeared.

She searched for *koura* for an hour, and found enough to

satisfy her. She made a small fire by the stream and steamed the crayfish in wet moss, eating them as they cooked. Max made small forays up the slopes behind her, sniffing through the tussock. He caught a rabbit, and lay happily eating it.

Alexa sat, her hunger satisfied, and stared beyond to the far side of the lake. The mountains seemed steeper there, impenetrable; she had never attempted to go beyond this stream tumbling into the gorge. She looked up, throwing her head back, following the jagged rim of peaks marching around the valley. What lay beyond them? Was she looking towards the Pacific — or back towards the homestead? She lay and mused. It was the first time she had wondered what lay beyond the lake.

There was a soft, excited chirring, and she saw with joy that the otters had returned. They had caught a small eel and were busy eating it with delicate paws and sharp, tiny teeth. For a long time, they sat and preened themselves like the cats on Marty's back step after getting the scraps. When they were done, they turned and looked directly at her.

So still did they sit now, so quiet were their whiskers, and so intently did they stare, it seemed to Alexa they were trying to tell her something. When they moved and swam slowly away from her, looking back at her with the same sharp stare, she could only follow. She saw they were leading her across the stream and around the far side of the lake where she had never been. The sun was high over the wall of mountains, and the facing cliffs were deep in shadow now. She looked back at her little part of the beach, saw Hobo grazing, bathed in the sunlight. But she followed the otters.

She thought it was odd the way they had become serious in their movements. She could hardly think of them as animals . . . She never considered questioning following them; it was so obvious what they asked of her.

For a long time, the otters led her along the cold shore, over rocks and through tangled tussock, through fingers of beech forest touching the water, over vines and through fern-shrouded boulders. Moss hung thick and green on the trees and stones, and the forest seemed silent and wet here. The snow was deep in places and crusted over, so the otters could run lightly in their funny, swaying hump-backed way along the smooth surface. They made no noise except for the whisper of their heavy tails on the hard snow. Alexa pushed after them.

After a time, it seemed the way was steeper, and they pulled further and further away from the shore. Sometimes they went through forest so thick she could not even see the water, and the beautiful otters slid and slipped through ferns and vines, half-hidden and silent. Max followed close at Alexa's heels, not foraging for smells as he usually did, as if he could sense something new here. Where were they leading her?

Now she knew they were climbing. They had left the lakeside completely behind and were climbing up through a forest. It was strange to see the otters so far from their lake, blending in with the soft browns and greens and dappled leaves of the forest floor. At times they seemed mere extensions of light filtering down through the sun-touched leaves on to the snow-pocketed, vine-tangled floor. They moved surely and steadily, keeping several lengths ahead of her, twisting and turning their long bodies with lightning speed and grace around black trees and great round boulders cloaked in moss.

When they broke clear of the forest at last, Alexa had to stop for breath, and the otters seemed to anticipate this, and remained crouching in the shelter of the forest edge. She was high up on a mountainside now, and above her was sparse tussock growing in the rocks and schist slides. She looked back at the otters. For the first time, they seemed to hesitate, and she saw it was because they did not like this open space so far from water. They hugged the forest still, watching her as if to see what she would do next. She looked above her and saw that what had seemed impassable mountains were marked here and there by saddles and passes in the ranges, and that she could climb to them without too much trouble.

Was that why she had come? Was this what the otters had brought her this far for? She shook her head, puzzled, looking from the otters to the saddle spanning the sky above her. It pulled her, that pass; the fact she knew she could get there, and she was so close, compelled her to go on. She turned and began to climb, the snow was thinner here. Max followed, still close at her heels. After a few minutes, she stopped and looked back: the otters had gone.

The clear cut of the saddle across the blue sky called her. It seemed so close, but it felt as if she climbed forever. Once she stopped and looked back, and found she was high above the forests, high above the lake. It looked as she had seen it that first night, ethereal, blue, untouched. But she had touched it; it was in her, a part of her.

She could see the white-rimmed shore curving around, sometimes laced with swamp and rushes and raupo where the pukekos hid their nests, sometimes shadowed by twisted giant beeches and sometimes bright and clear with shining sand. She looked way down, saw the tiny rock-slide where her cave was, with a thin tendril of smoke threading the air. She saw the dark forest behind where Max had fought the boar.

A few minutes more and she had reached the saddle-top. Her heart pounded in her and the blood raced in her veins. She looked back over the valley, saw it all, opened her arms and stood completely filled with the cold and wind and freedom of the place. This is mine! She cried inside. I did it! I made it happen! All by myself!

She wanted to call out, hear her voice fill the mountains, drift down echoes over the lake, cause the otters to stop in their playing and listen, bright eyes gleaming. She stuck her hands deep into her pockets and stood, drinking in the air. She felt a lump in one pocket; her hand closed around something, and she pulled it out.

It was the red scarf! The red scarf Billy had given her in town the day before he'd left on the muster! She drew it through her fingers, fascinated. She had forgotten all about it. It was muddy and wrinkled but still the soft shimmering of the material came through, and the bright redness of it seared through the snow and rock around her. How brilliant it was against the snow! Billy had given it to her. What had he said? Something funny, when he'd given it to her — she couldn't remember. She saw an old dry stick lying in the shale and stooped to pick it up. She tied the scarf on to one end and jammed the other triumphantly into the ground. It caught between two stones and stood strongly, the red scarf whipping in the wind. She laughed aloud, throwing back her head.

'Here I am!' she cried, and the call flew from crag to ridge, fell from cliffs down, down, echoing into the lake. 'Here I am! Here I am!'

She felt as the discoverer of a new land must have felt, or the discoverer of a lost tribe of people, or even someone who had just discovered an idea. As if the world suddenly were bigger, and because she was a part of it, as if she were bigger, too. And suddenly, it *was* a discovery that came to her. Suddenly, she knew why she had come.

It had seemed, back at the homestead, as if everything were a fight. She had fought her mother because it made her angry to see her tied to baby and kitchen. And she fought her father, Jim, because his ideas seemed so set and narrow and hemmed her in. And Tod — why had she begun to fight Tod? They had always been friends as children, but when he'd come back from school, suddenly, it had all changed. It was as if he'd challenged her at every turn, left her out of his life on purpose, making her feel she was too young or not experienced enough.

'But he wasn't, really,' she said, aloud. 'It's just that he wants to do different things from me, and just because we *used* to do everything together, I guess I figured we still had to. We're just going different ways, I reckon.'

She felt so excited, she stood again. She knew that terrible restless feeling that had tormented her for months was gone, and that she could see more clearly. Perhaps people would not agree with everything she'd set herself to do — but that was not a problem. The important thing was to find her place in the world, and go strongly out from there.

At that moment she felt capable of doing anything! She

could even go to the pictures with Clive and have fun. It didn't mean more than that. Nothing could hold her back — nothing except measuring herself against other people, when instead she should let them live their own lives and respect them for that.

Suddenly, she remembered what Billy had said when he had given her the red scarf.

'It's for when you want the world to see you,' he'd said. She remembered now. 'It's for when you want to walk out and say 'Here I am!'

And she had shouted that, just minutes before. 'Here I am! Here I am!'

Was she ready now? Ready to go back? Ready to be part of the world she came from? Yes. She held her breath, thinking. Yes. She was ready. She had come on her muster, her own private adventure. And now it was time to go home.

For the first time since she'd climbed to the saddle she turned and looked out at what lay beyond the hidden valley. The lake was behind her. In front, spread out below her forever, was the vast white high country. She stared as far out as she could and saw at last the distant, almost mirage-like gleam of the ocean. And then she brought her eyes closer and closer in, over the endless hills of snow and tussock, over the pockets of scrub, closer and closer till she saw a narrow rushing river winding its way through a shallow gorge. The river seemed almost at the foot of the mountain she stood on. And there was something, something . . .

Something there, moving. A small figure. A tiny thread of smoke. A dog . . .

12

IT WAS DARK in the forest, and Tod slept far into the morning. The sun which dappled down on him through the stirring tops of the beeches finally woke him. He lay staring around him. The forest was transformed. The sun streamed through breaks above him, lighting patches of fern or tangles of creepers magically. Invisible in the depths of the green mass beyond him came the stirrings of birds, and their single cries filtered down to him clear and pure as the sun. Above him a fantail glinted in the light, flitting from branch to vine, flicking its tail, twittering. He shrugged out of his sleeping bag and blankets, pushing aside the piles of moss. Rose crawled out with him.

The first thing he did was check his pack. As he had feared, the radio had been crushed by the horse falling on it during the avalanche. He fiddled with it, but saw it was useless. He tried to remember when was the last time he'd contacted Billy. It had to have been quite a while ago. He knew fairly well where he was, though, and since he'd gone over the route with Billy before he'd left, he was not worried. They would be sending a plane to search near here soon enough.

He pushed out of the forest to the narrow river bank. The sun was bright and warm; the day filled him with energy. He was starving. He ran back, dragged out his food pack, and built a fire on a flat shelf of sand. Rose sniffed happily in the thickets. She, too, was grateful for the warmth after the previous day's cold and snow. He thrust a tin of sardines into the flame, and put his billy on. While it heated, he took his binoculars and went out to a rise in the bend of the river.

He studied the narrow water for some time. It was deep and violent, rushing with force through its narrow bed. Rocks stuck above the water in places. No matter how far up or down he looked, the river seemed the same: impassable. He sighed and surveyed the mountains beyond through his binoculars. They looked equally discouraging.

There must be a way to get through them, he thought. The day seemed endless to him, and he was rested and full of energy. There was food heating for him in the fire. Anything was possible. Eagerly, he scanned the ridges that towered beyond the river.

They began to take on shape, gain characteristics, offer possible access. Here, a narrow fissure with plenty of footholds, there a ledge and a gentle slope beyond it. And look — there! A broad saddle, looking accessible from the north by the long sweep of a spur like a finger reaching out... He studied it carefully through the binoculars, planning his ascent. The saddle cut the brilliant line of blue with the sparkle of its own white snow. It took his breath away, and he squinted at it. Over that saddle, he knew, he would see the lake. The map showed him that. He squinted, blinked his eyes in the glare. Something pierced into the blue from the middle of that curved saddle. A tree? No tree could survive up there! He took the binoculars away, shook his head, and looked again. There *was* something there! A stick? What was a stick doing stuck up there . . .

And on the stick he could see something fluttering. Something long, and bright red. The glare burned into his eyes. Red! Like a flag! It was a flag, there on the saddle. No, not a flag! Suddenly he knew, and whooped in incredulous joy. It was the red scarf! Alexa's red scarf. She had waved it at him as they rode away on the first morning of the muster. And it was now flying high over the great walls of rock and snow, red and proud and strong. She was up there, and he would find her, and only the river lay between them.

The river. He could see no way to cross it, no way of bridging it. Yet he must cross it. It was cold, fed by ice and snow, and fast, propelled by the mountains and cutting deep

138

through this gorge. He didn't have a rope or he might have, if he were lucky, been able to throw one across and have it catch hold on the other side. He considered fashioning one from vines. But now, hunger caught him, and he turned back to his fire, deep in thought.

He sat eating out of the hot tin by the river bank. He stared out across the rushing white river. Not far from where he sat, he noticed that a small portion of the far bank seemed to slope gradually into the water, rather than falling in a sharp drop. He wandered down to study it. Yes, he was sure — about half-way across at this point, the water seemed calmer, the bottom less rocky. The roar of the water was very loud and filled his whole head.

Calmly, he went back to Nelson, re-packed him. Nelson was a good, strong swimmer, he knew. If he could manage to hold on to the horse, he would have a good chance of getting across. He felt oddly detached from the knowledge that this crossing would be extremely dangerous, and that there was a chance he would drown. He didn't care. In his mind was the image of the oval lake lying tiny and serene in the midst of those awesome ranges of rock and snow and mist. Alexa was there.

Tod led the horse to the shoreline and called to Rose. He untied one rein and re-tied it to the other, so there was a long line trailing out behind the horse. He wrapped it firmly around his wrist and hand. Without hesitating, he called to the horse, flicking the strap. Rose plunged in ahead, and Nelson, with a shrill whinny, crashed chest-deep into the swirling roar.

Instantly the cold claimed him. The roar silenced. His body curled and tightened into a ball, and he felt the burn of cold water enter him until all was blackness. For all eternity, all was cold and water and movement, being thrown up and down, turned under.

Something hard bashed his shoulder, jerking his body, causing him to uncurl, thrash, strain for the surface. In a dream, the water gave in for a second and he gasped for air. Beside him, the horse was swept, hooves churning, and he

139

caught a flash of white-rimmed eyes and deep red nostrils. He curled again, the river took him, he was dashed against the horse's body.

He could not breathe, and he knew it now. His mind came alive. He forced himself to want to breathe. It was mad, this river; it was eating him alive. He would not let it! But the water had strong tentacles. It pulled him and swept him down, down. He fought now. He could not beat it, but he wouldn't give in. Go with it. He relaxed, turned his body with the current. How cold it was. There was never such cold. He could not see. It was all black. He knew he hit something, hard, but he could not feel anything except the blackness ever deeper and closing around him . . .

For a long time Alexa stood on the saddle, her eyes burning in the wind with the strain of watching the tiny figure below her. She hung in balance. Behind her lay the valley, and there, down there was Tod. She knew it was Tod. It had to be, although she was not sure how she knew. There was only the vague form of dark horse, dark dog, and human on the snow-covered bank of the river. The little figure built a fire, sat for a long time, walked along the riverbank. She wondered if he had seen the scarf. Twice she reached up to pull it down, and twice she squatted down again, to watch.

If it were Tod, what was he doing there, all alone? He must have come to find her! But how would he have known . . . Billy! The thought flashed through her, and with it, an instant, gut-wrenching feeling of betrayal. Had Billy *told* Tod where she was? She squirmed forward, knowing that the figure could not see her, hidden as she was on the saddle's edge behind some rocks. She remembered the map, and how she had perhaps given herself away by showing interest in the lake — could Tod have put it all together? Maybe Billy hadn't told him anything, after all.

She lay watching the wild, snow-swollen river; there was no way they could cross, so she was safe. Her valley lay protected behind her. When she was ready, she would go down the mountain to stand on the bank. Perhaps they could shout across at each other. It was entirely possible it was not Tod, after all, her reason told her. Perhaps just a lone musterer, or someone passing through the station . . .

So when she watched the figure pack up the horse, lead him to the edge, and plunge in, her mind at first would not let her accept what she saw. When it did, her body responded, leaping up and out, her legs like pistons pushing her down the steep slope, bounding over rocks, sliding on her bottom down the patches of snow and the bare schist slides. It *was* Tod! No one — *no one* — would do that, attempt something crazy like that, except Tod. In fear and sudden joy she zig-zagged down, until she hit the first straggling patches of bush. The going became more intricate; she wove herself in and out among the twisted alpine shrubs, leaping over dead logs and finally entering the stunted forest that descended to the shore. She could no longer see the river, but with every leap of her she could hear the roar, louder and louder, and her fear became acute.

They could never survive that river! No one could manage to manoeuvre in that intensity of cold, avoid those treacherous rocks. Her breath sobbed deep in her chest. She would find him bashed and bloody far down the rapids — or perhaps she would never find him. There were great snags hidden under those currents, which could catch him and hold him there forever in the black cold. She fairly flew through the tangled forest, Max leaping beside her. When Alexa slammed through the last mass of bushes at the edge of the forest, she stopped. The river lay in front of her, rushing past her with a sound that utterly cowed her. She darted her eyes up and down; nowhere was there the head of a horse or man. Nothing. Exhausted, her breath returning raggedly to her, her chest burning and her legs trembling from the jarring run down the mountain, she could only cry. Beside her Max whimpered.

Something sharp was sticking into him. It pushed past the blackness and the cold. His arm was being torn from him. He struggled feebly. Water entered his mouth and eyes; he fought it off. He could not bear the sharpness pressing against him. He could not stand the pull against his arm. He struck out with his body, kicking his legs. At once the sharpness left and pressure on his arm let up. Once more the water closed around him, but it felt softer, like gentler waves. His cheek scraped roughness; once more his wrist burned and pulled. He found he could open his eyes. He could breathe! He was like rubber, waving in the shallow current, his cheek dug into the coarse sand. He retched once, suddenly. Everything swirled around him and he felt like slipping back, back into that rushing nothingness. But something held him. The horse. Yes. He was tied to the horse. And something was pawing at him, from all sides. He moaned and struggled against it. More pawing, and something . . . his name? His name? How could that be? He moaned and retched again, feeling his mouth fill with water.

Something was dragging him against the hard sand. It was too hard; it did not move and swirl about him like the river. He curled, but the pawing would not stop. Why did it keep calling him? Tod! Tod!

This time the pawing did not bother him so much. He was too tired, and it was warm now. Something was warm on him. He drank in air. Good. Good. He felt like opening his eyes, and when he did, a face swam in at him. A dirty, thin face, with big dark staring eyes. A face rimmed with matted brown hair. He stared. The face topped a hideous body of stinking black hair which trailed, matted with leaves and sticks and mud, into the snow. Below the shapeless, hairy body were two legs in torn pants, and boots caked with mud. He moaned and closed his eyes. A warm wetness covered his face and he forced himself up. Two dogs. Rose. Good. It was Rose. But what — Max! It was Max! But if that was Max, was that — *Alexa*?!

She called and called him. He seemed only to flop his head in her hands and moan, and occasionally water would trickle from his mouth. That was good, she knew. He was breathing, but shivering violently. She laid him carefully on the sand and flew into the forest, ripping great handfuls of moss and leaves, the driest she could find. She threw the goat carcass over him, oblivious to her own cold. She piled the moss around him. Frantically, she searched every pocket she had. There *had* to be a match! She knew she hadn't used them all up! There! She got a small fire going at once, feeding it with twigs from the forest edge. Then, kneeling, she pulled off as many wet clothes as she could and began to rub the blue skin.

He revived quickly after that. She wrapped the pelt fur-side in around him, giving him also her jersey.

The sun still beat down on them. It might have been early afternoon, but she was not sure. She sat next to him and fed the fire. At last he sat up and looked at her.

'I could see you, up there,' she said, jerking her head towards the mountain behind them. 'As soon as you went in the river, I knew it was you!' She didn't know how else to start.

'Well, I didn't know who *you* were!' said Tod, plucking at the goat fur. They looked at each other, and when they laughed, it was as if all the sunshine in the world suddenly filled them up. Suddenly, they could not stop talking.

'Dad told me to stay on the muster, but I just reckoned I knew where you were, eh, so here I am!' he said brightly, to hide what was piling up in his chest.

'You couldn't have just guessed!' she cried, curiously aggravated. 'Anyway, why didn't you let Dad know?'

'Well, I tried,' Tod answered. But he knew he hadn't tried very hard.

'It was just — that I *knew* where you'd be —' he continued. 'I thought about that map, you know, and how you'd said about otters . . .'

He found himself reluctant to explain *why* he had felt compelled to come looking for her. He waited for her to ask, but she did not. Instead, she seemed to be looking at him with a strange light in her eyes.

'I'm glad!' she cried suddenly, fiercely. 'I'm glad *you* came, and not anyone else. And besides, I was ready to leave . . .'

'I saw your flag.' He watched her face. 'Did you find the lake? Did you?'

143

She did not answer him but stuck some more sticks into the fire.

'Billy said you wouldn't want me here,' Tod muttered after a time. She looked up, surprised.

'But . . . I *am* glad,' she said, as surprised herself as he was. Yesterday, it would not have been so. Perhaps even that morning, as she had sat in the sun drawing. But Tod had come to find her, alone, against Jim's wishes, for some reason that she would not understand.

'Dad didn't want you to, eh?' she said, almost to herself. 'But you did anyway.'

'I knew where you were.' He said it simply; it seemed the best reason. They smiled at each other. Alexa felt full of love. Here was Tod, who knew her so well. He had come a long way, through snow and through that crazy river, to find her, simply because he *knew* she would be there.

'I bet no one else would ever believe that I could do that,' she said. It was vague, but he did not question her. He knew it meant she *had* found her lake, and maybe even the otters. He was proud of her.

She left him to check the horse. Nelson greeted her as he always did, as if she had never been gone, as if he had never been on a fantastic journey through an avalanche and a wild river. He butted her coat, hoping for a barley sugar. She cradled his head in her arms and held him. Nelson. Nelson. Tod had cared for him well. She turned back to her brother.

'Did Billy figure where I was, and tell you?' she asked abruptly. He looked at her in surprise.

'No, I figured it,' he said. 'It *was* something Billy said, started me thinking, though — about otters.' He looked at her, fearing he might have trod on private ground. But she only listened impassively. 'Then I remembered that night I showed you my map — you know? An' you kept tracin' your finger up to the corner, to this wee lake —'

Alexa kicked up the fire to get it burning higher. Tod went on, musing: 'Funny, eh. Billy sort of *let* me go, to look for you I mean. Dad sure wouldn't have! I *knew* where you were, an' I reckoned I would rescue you —' He stopped, and grinned at

144

her. 'But it was me that needed the rescuing, eh!'

'You're the only person in the whole world who would have tried a crazy daft thing like crossing that river all by yourself, and *do* it!' There was such pride in her voice that Tod turned away confused.

So Billy was not the only one who believed in her, who believed in stories and secrets and *having to do what you have to do!* she thought wildly. Tod had started out on a hunch, a tiny rumour in his heart. And Billy had known all along. Of course he had let Tod go! Better to try to stop a midwinter storm in these mountains! But even more, he knew Tod would find her, and he must have known, too, that it would create a new bond between them, stronger than any they'd ever had.

Tod huddled shivering in the pelt. His clothes, still damp, were spread close to the fire. He was not going to get enough warmth from that pelt, especially if a wind came up.

He coughed. She watched him, worried. She was beginning to feel cold, even in the sun, and Tod was still damp. She needed the blankets. They might have to spend another night here.

'I have to go back,' she said at last. He didn't ask where, but waited for her to continue.

'I have some blankets, and more matches, and ... things,' she hesitated. 'Could you manage here a few hours?'

'It's not that much different from gettin' soaked in the snow and wind all day, on a muster, eh!' he grinned at her. She grinned back. He would be all right. She left a pile of dead sticks for the fire and started back up the mountain.

It took her more than an hour to get back. She left Max with Tod and Rose. It was funny to trudge along the lake shore now, preparing to leave. She felt she had been there many years. She hopped over the streams, traversed the swamp, pushed through the patches of forest, and walked at last along the sandy edge toward the cave. Everything was there. Hobo greeted her with a whicker. It took five minutes to gather the blankets and knife, the extra matches, the pad of paper and pencils. Was that all she had left here? She left it in a small pile rolled in the blanket by Hobo, and went to stand on the lake edge.

The day was still clean and pure with sunlight. Even during the time she had been gone that morning, the warmth had begun to melt the snow in patches, so now large areas of tussock and earth showed through again. The ice at the shoreline was wet and dripped slowly down into the lake. She felt unutterably sad.

It was not that she wanted to stay. In fact, she had noticed herself anticipating her return to the homestead as she had climbed back down into the valley. She did not know exactly why she felt sad. She thought, it must be that something which could only happen once was over. And I will never see my otters again.

But as she sat on her favourite rock in the sun, the lake water stirred and whispered at her in that familiar way, and she felt a thrill run through her whole body. Once again, the lake broke and released its treasured secret. Once again, she saw him. There was only the one now, as he had first come to her. There was only the one, the otter who had greeted her, fed her, woken her from her snow-sleep, shared his friend with her, and led her up the final mountain to her brother. He was here, lilting weightless in the clear depths, watching her with his ageless eyes.

He willed her to close her eyes. She did. He willed her to sit perfect and quiet; she did. He willed her breathing to come to her as from a great distance, so she would make no sound, and all this she did. And in the sun, he came slipping out of the lake and quietly, softly, he came up the white beach towards her. She opened her eyes and breathed again. Her leg felt on fire, and she saw that he was there beside it, almost touching. She could see every oiled and sleek hair on his warm brown body. She saw the tiny ears folded inside themselves to keep the water out, saw the exquisite long-fingered black paws, saw the sensitive face moving, sensing her, smelling, hearing her. He was saying goodbye to her.

Slowly, unafraid, she reached out and put her hand on the otter. Instantly, she felt the trilling of life under her fingers.

146

She felt the life blood coursing through the veins to the strong animal heart, felt the muscles fluttering and adjusting, felt the heart beating, the fur stirring. She felt the warm breathing of the otter on her fingers, felt the tremor of stiff whiskers, saw he was sniffing her, taking in her scent as fully as she was taking in his feel.

The otter stretched under her hand, so it was firmer on his back, and placing his agile, hand-like paw on her leg he came to his full height and stared deep into her face. For a moment, they were perfectly balanced and still.

And then he was gone. Her hand slipped down, the body under it darted, sure and strong, back to the lake. Without looking back, the otter chirred deep in his throat, slid into a mass of delicate green weed, and disappeared into the depthless blue.

Later, high up the far slope, she turned and looked back. Hobo laboured beside her, his bad leg trembling slightly on the shale. It was slow going. Already the sun had reached the rim of her valley. By the time she reached the saddle-top, it was dark behind her, and the land stretched out beyond the rushing river was heavy and long in golden light and shadow. There was no need for her to turn and stare back the way she had come. She knew what she had left, and she had made her farewell. For the first time, she was aware she had been squeezing something in her hand ever since she had left the lake. Slowly, painfully, she opened her hand on the windy saddle. It was a small white pebble, perfect and oval. It was from the place near her rock where the otter had stood. It had been still wet from his body when she had picked it up, but now it was hot from being held tightly for more than an hour. She slipped it into her pocket. She turned, lifted the red scarf from its pole in the snow, and started down the mountain.

The roar of the river could not hide the rhythmic beat of the helicopter. She felt its slow approach long before she could see it coming from the direction of the setting sun. Below her, Tod had built the fire to a blaze on the broad flat bank, and he was standing wrapped in the hideous goat pelt, waiting for

147

his sister and the helicopter. Slowly, with the injured horse, she descended to the waiting search team.

Distant, disjointed events broke through the numbness and exhaustion of the following hours. Along with Tod she had been greeted, bundled warm and tight into the helicopter, reassured that Hobo and Nelson would be lifted out early the next morning and given something warm to drink. She remembered later that she'd thought it strange how they'd fed her — as if she had not eaten for a long, long time. Talk swirled around her, but she saw Tod was not among the speakers. Nameless faces, the crackling of the control board and radio, and the steady rhythm of the helicopter lulled her dreamless into a weightless state of limbo between sleep and waking.

But once, the helicopter banked sharply and curved around to head back towards the homestead, and suddenly, below her, for one instant, she saw the stars captured in a tiny point of utter black nestled deep inside the mountains. Tod saw it, too. The warmth from each of them flowed into the other as they leaned close to look down into that star-filled lake.

She took her white pebble from her pocket and gave it to him.

'What is it?' he asked, his voice low and groggy with exhaustion.

'It's the sort of stone an otter might play with,' she answered him.

13

THERE WAS SNOW now at the homestead, dusting the gentle hills of the lower station. Early that morning the musterers had brought the sheep in, and now they could be seen everywhere, dotting the bare hills, their coats dingy and dark against the night's new snow. It was now late afternoon on a grey day; it looked like mid-winter, cold and lonely and barren. The men were packing up, going back to their winter homes, their families in Kaikoura and Culverden. The pack and riding horses were turned loose in the big paddock, the dogs kennelled or tied in the back of pick-ups, waiting alert and patient.

The men had a final cup of tea in Marty's kitchen, and the small warm room steamed with damp wool jerseys and swam in the blue fog of tobacco smoke. The kettle screamed on the stove, the pot was filled and re-filled, and the room hummed with the low contented murmur of tired men. Tod was with them, leaning his elbows with the others on the table. One by one, the men left, saying their goodbyes, heaving a final piece of gear into their truck beds. The yard rang with the spurting and coughing of old motors.

Billy Turoa checked under the bonnet of his truck. He threw an old coat in the back as a bed for the dog; Alexa leaned against the fence and watched. She and Tod had been back five days now. She had waited for Billy's return; she had something for him. She waited until he was in the cab, coaxing the truck to start. When she handed him the drawings through the window, they looked at each other silently: two people sharing something special. He smoothed his rough gnarled hand over the paper, now dirty and wrinkled with water, smudged, and covered with the drawings of a place they both knew. The deep brown eyes that stared into her own held her powerfully, as those other brown eyes had, watching her from a small, whiskered face . . .

There seemed nothing to say. It did not bother either of them. Billy would go; he would be back. But the old man reached out and touched gently the red scarf she wore around her neck. It was as close as he had ever come to embracing her. He rolled up the window; the engine caught, fired once, and the truck rolled crunching on the cold gravel out the gate.

Tod had come out now, too, and stood with Alexa as Billy drove off.

'Clive's come over,' he said to her.

'Oh, yeah? Why'd he come?'

'Thought somebody'd need a lift, I guess . . . that's what he told me,' said Tod, nonchalant. He grinned at her. She grinned back. She thought it would be nice to see Clive. She wandered around the yard. She was tired: they'd made her and Tod stay in bed for three days and most of yesterday, and she was still groggy.

Jim came out from a shed. When he saw her, he smiled and came towards her, trailing a bridle that needed mending.

'Up and about, eh?' he said, letting his arm fold over her shoulders. He'd done that when she was very young. She leaned against him. Max, who had been curled in the dirt near the door, trotted up. Jim automatically put his hand on the big golden head, as he did with all his dogs. Alexa watched him, and Jim laughed, embarrassed.

'Useless mutt!' he said. 'But if you fought off a boar, you can't be such a sook, eh?' He straightened and rolled up the straps of the bridle in his hand. 'Still no good with sheep, I suppose?' he continued.

Alexa caught her breath, fought the fear. It was coming,

150

then: the final decision about Max. She could not see the brightness of her father's eyes.

'No good,' she said, strongly, waiting.

'Lucky thing, eh. Couldn't let you keep him, if he was — I'd have to take him back,' said Jim. He walked towards the kitchen. Her breath released in a small huff. That was that, then.

She raced in to tell Tod, but when she ran instead into Clive as he was wandering across the yard, she found herself telling him, her words tumbling one over the other in her excitement. He stared at her. He hadn't seen her since that day in town, and here she was, after being lost for four days in a blizzard. She was very thin, her skin was darkened by wind and sun. He had forgotten how tall she was, and how deliberately she moved, and how solemn her face was. But there was something else now — as if she had something inside her that made her glow . . . He couldn't think what to say to her, so could only stare. At last he blurted: 'I came to see you.'

'I know,' she answered. She watched him, curious.

'Well, I figured — you'd be bored now at home so do you want to go to town maybe . . . to the pictures?'

'OK,' she replied, without hesitation.

But now she wanted to be around Marty. Each morning since she had been back, she had woken up with a dull panicky feeling, knowing how distressed Jim and Marty had been when they thought she was lost. Early in the morning, alone, the knowledge of all the trouble she had caused would slide over her in a painful wash. The ache of this would fade if she stayed in Marty's presence, or sat near Jim in the evening while he went over the books in the study. She wished it would go away. She trusted Tod, but still, even though he knew, she could not speak of it to him.

She sat at the kitchen table. Marty was washing up the last cups from tea; all the men had left the room. Alexa picked up the baby. This time it felt vibrant and warm, trembling with life like the firm smooth body of the otter.

'Mum — remember when we talked, the other night, before

151

I left . . . got lost?' she said. Marty nodded.

'Remember you said you thought I'd go away? I just wanted you to know, if I *do*, it's not 'cause I hate it here. It's just that, well, I want to learn about *everything*! I sort of learned some things, when I was lost . . . and I want to see if they *work*. You know?'

Marty turned to look into her daughter's face. So serious, always so serious! But now there was another emotion written across it — happiness — she could see she was happy. Those four long days she had been gone — what *had* happened to her daughter?

'Did you see Clive?' she said softly.

'Yes, he wants me to go to town tonight, to the pictures.'

It was a straightforward statement. Marty thought, why am *I* the one who feels flustered? Her first date! She isn't worried at all!

'As long as you're back by ten,' she said, automatically. Alexa was growing up so quickly! What had happened out there, in the snow, in those awful bare mountains? Her intuition was more acute than Jim's; she knew there was a change in their daughter. Perhaps one day Alexa would feel she could tell her about it.

Alexa left the kitchen and went to search for Tod. She found him watching television. He was draped over the couch, a pillow propped behind his head. He had pulled blankets over himself from head to toe, for he still shook sometimes from the chill he'd got in the river. She sat on the arm of the couch.

'Dad's officially given me Max,' she announced. He looked up and grinned.

'That's great, eh!' he cried. 'But I never really thought he'd get rid of him. He could see how much you loved him.'

She shrugged.

'Dad's good — I think he just gets scared, eh. He gets scared about money, an' the station. As he sees it, everything here must be used to the full, otherwise it puts demands elsewhere.' He said the last pensively and with a deep voice. Tod would never leave, she thought. He would work himself old like Jim had, work until his face was indistinguishable from the dry and windy land it looked upon.

'How are you?' Tod's voice broke into her mood, and she started.

'Oh, Tod! If only you knew — if I could just *tell* you *everything* that happened — but I can't. I can hardly straighten it all out inside!' she blurted out.

'You'll get it straight, Lex,' Tod said softly. He paused, then, 'You going to break Clive's heart?' he baited her.

Alexa coloured slightly. 'I *like* Clive,' she answered simply.

'He's talking about getting land of his own one of these days. I bet he'll want a wife then!'

Alexa knew he was teasing her, half-seriously. She knew what it was like; it happened to girls on other stations. A young man would hang around, getting to know the family, waiting for the girl to grow up, waiting for his money to build enough so he could get his section, put up a house . . .

'Tod, you know I'm not going to marry Clive. You know I probably won't marry anyone — not here, at least. I feel like I have all these things I've got to do, like I don't have enough time — I feel like I have things to say.' She spoke all this slowly and quietly, and in such a serious tone Tod felt subdued. This was the Alexa that was not part of him, of his home. This was the sudden rush of foreign air that came into the room with her, the air from places he would never, never see.

'Well, I'm glad,' he answered her. He meant it. 'Just bring me back a pebble, a little pebble from all those places you reckon you'll get to, eh!'

It was funny, he thought later, how she'd hugged him. Gratefully. That was it. Like he'd said something special. And then she'd left the room before he had a chance to hug her back.

Later that evening Clive was waiting for her in the kitchen.

'You ready?' she said. He nodded. They walked out to the truck. It was just dusk as they started off. They didn't know what was playing in town. The street glowed orange from street lights, and the neon sign at the takeaway had one letter out dead. The dairy was crowded with boys hanging around the front of the window, leaning against old Tip-Top ice-cream signs, eating chips from greasy bags.

Clive and Alexa wandered slowly down the street, past the hardware store and the bank and the bakery, until they reached the cinema. A horror movie was showing. They both groaned, and laughed, and by common consent turned and sat on the peeling bench in front of the bank. They were silent, neither knowing how to break the silence.

'So — your Dad'll take you next year, for sure, on muster, eh! If you roughed it four days alone, I reckon you could make it on a muster!' Clive said this brightly to hide his unease, but she caught the admiration in his voice.

'He'd never want me there — but it doesn't matter. I don't think I'll want to go next time,' she said. She didn't expect him to understand her.

'What was it like for you — out there?' he asked her suddenly, his voice soft. She looked at him curiously. He seemed to really want to know. Would it hurt to tell him? Well maybe she would tell him a *little* . . .

'It filled me up,' she answered him, and to her amazement, he accepted it as a reply and waited for her to continue. 'It was sometimes just all wind and when it snowed, it was like there was nothing alive to see, but I knew it was all there, hidden —' As she spoke, the words came easier, and she painted a world of rock and snow, of wind and hawks hanging above her, of the wild song of the pipit and the scream of the kea. She filled the mountains with tussock for him, made him feel the wind sharp on his face, made him lean low over the horse's neck as it pulled up a spur. He listened and his eyes glowed; he held his broken wrist in his hand as if willing it to heal faster so he could go out once more into the high country that was the only place he felt at home. And here was this strange dark girl, who wasn't really a girl but like no woman he'd ever met, telling him about what he loved and knew in words he would never have thought of for himself, but understood perfectly. Her face stayed quite still

154

as she spoke, but the tone of her voice was full and her eyes glowed, even in the dim light of the street. He wanted to touch her face, but shyness held him back.

They walked down past the dairy and out on to the football field. She had stopped talking.

'I'll tell you something,' she whispered to him suddenly. It was so dark and quiet on the football field. In the cold air the stars seemed to crackle above them, so bright were they. 'A secret,' she said.

It was all right. He wouldn't believe her, but she wanted to tell him. She wanted to hear herself speak the words to another human being. He liked her; she felt warm with him because he was undemanding and uncomplicated. And it was all right to tell him because he would never call her up again, or try to see her. He wanted someone like himself, like her mother . . .

'I didn't get lost,' she said. 'I went out on purpose. I knew exactly where I was going. I was sometimes very afraid. But I was looking for something. And I found it.' She paused briefly. 'I found an otter in a lake, way in the mountains.'

How cool the words sounded in the bright darkness of the field by the road. It was like a wonderful, cool breeze at the end of a hot summer, those words falling out into the world. He would think her silly now, a dumb kid, she thought. He would think she had seen things, up there alone for four days.

But despite himself, forever after, he would remember that strange girl, and how she'd told him about the mountains and told him she'd seen an otter. And whenever after that he came across a hidden tarn or tiny lake as he mustered or mended fences, he would find himself staring into the clear deep water, watching for a ripple, a whisper of movement from deep within, only half-aware that he watched for the otter to come.

The wind picked up on the exposed field, and they walked back. They ate hamburgers in the truck as he drove her home, saying little. Once, she caught his eye and he smiled at her. And Alexa smiled back, and she thought of all she had found.

The night was bright black and cold. On the surface of the little lake the stars lay peacefully, so still was the water. The otter surfaced from very deep, without warning. He surveyed the shore but the girl had gone. He was content. He had just eaten an eel, and had lain curled against the other otter on the rocks. And then quietly, as he had come, he sank beneath the black surface again. The stars fell together once more on the water. Nothing moved.